Snuffing the fuse in a powder-keg city of hate

Scars of mortar shells pockmarked the road and countryside as The Executioner gunned the Fiat back toward Beirut.

Bolan and his Israeli companion met no military traffic and none of the sporadic fighting that peppered the night, only a few pedestrians heading the other way, refugees from the holocaust.

The thunder and lightning of war grew fierce as the vehicle drew closer to the city.

"It is difficult to believe," commented the Mossad agent, "that Beirut was not long ago known as the Paris of the Mediterranean."

The Executioner eyed the vista beyond the windshield as flares arced into the sky. Then he spoke.

"It looks like Nam."

MACK BOLAN
The Executioner

DON PENDLETON's EXECUTIONER
MACK BOLAN
Beirut Payback

A GOLD EAGLE BOOK FROM
W🦅RLDWIDE

TORONTO • NEW YORK • LONDON • PARIS
AMSTERDAM • STOCKHOLM • HAMBURG
ATHENS • MILAN • TOKYO • SYDNEY

First edition July 1984

ISBN 0-373-61067-X

Special thanks and acknowledgment to
Stephen Mertz for his contributions to this work.

Printed in Canada

A foreign war is a scratch on the arm; a civil war is an ulcer which devours the vitals of a nation.

—*Victor Hugo*, Ninety-Three, *1879*

I know how it is in Beirut. I know how it's been in the latest fractured months, the city crushed by dark and terrible tides, its war no less everlasting than my own. I've been there. Inescapably I am the American soldier in Beirut.

—*Mack Bolan*

IN APPRECIATION

To the U.S. Marines in Beirut seen wearing
"The Executioner " headband on their helmets.
An appropriate badge of courage. Live large!

1

Mack Bolan melded with the violent shadows of war-torn midnight.

A night of hellfire for Beirut.

Golden-hued strobe flashes seared the dark Mediterranean sky like heat lightning, punctuating the steady rumble of impacting mortar and artillery shells inside the city not far to the north.

The Executioner waited, togged in combat black-suit. "Big Thunder," the stainless-steel .44 AutoMag, hung in quickdraw leather strapped low to his right hip. The silenced Beretta 93-R nestled snug in its speed rig beneath his left arm near a sheathed combat knife. Canvas pouches worn at his waist carried extra ammo for the handguns. A wire garrote, cigarette-pack-sized high-frequency radio transceiver and a lightweight array of hard punch munitions, plastique and grenades completed his gear, none of it cumbersome.

Bolan crouched silently, restless for action, in a grove of jasmine and olive trees along an uninhabited stretch of road. He had been waiting there for the past thirty minutes.

Too long, he decided abruptly.

He started to move out soundlessly on foot at a fast clip through the brush, parallel to but well in from the road, toward the city.

He would find his own transportation.

Traffic past this rendezvous point had been sparse during the wait: a rumbling government tank on its way into the fray; two troop carriers hurriedly redeploying Lebanese soldiers into Beirut from the mountains; an occasional civilian vehicle daring to travel on a night like this to escape the holocaust Beirut had become after another fractured ceasefire in this country's ongoing civil strife.

Tonight's hard punch into Lebanon held a very special meaning for Bolan.

Too many American lives had been sacrificed for this raging hellground in the quest for an elusive peace.

One U.S. serviceman lost would have been unacceptable to Bolan.

The figures on the balance sheet were written in red—the blood of U.S. Marines.

And The Executioner had come to settle the account with the cannibals who ran wild in a country less than four-fifths the size of Connecticut.

But even the gnawing gut urge to do something where his nation's military presence and diplomacy had failed took second priority to the mission's immediate objective. He was ready and willing to risk it all on the line one more time. And Bolan the realist did not kid himself for a single instant that this could not well be the last time, considering the odds. But, yeah, call it personal.

All the way.

A shabby five-year-old Fiat with one headlight approached Bolan's position.

The car braked off to the side of the road five hundred feet away and across from the grove of jasmine and olive. The driver killed the engine and headlight and waited.

Bolan paused in his withdrawal, remaining in deep shadow, and unleathered the AutoMag. Man and weapon probed the night for danger.

In the near distance, the noisy bombardment of Beirut continued unabated, as it had for hours. The ground trembled with the fury of war, even out here beyond the suburbs.

Nothing moved. Bolan and the car had the stretch of country road to themselves. Or so it seemed.

The nightfighter approached the vehicle with all the noise of a specter.

The driver concentrated on a point several hundred yards up the road from the grove where Bolan had waited.

The nightblitzer had not intended to meet his contact as planned. Too much danger of a trap. While the man at the steering wheel watched the point where Bolan should have been, the specter reached the driver's side of the car and pressed the muzzle of the awesome AutoMag against the man's left temple.

"There are two ways to die," Bolan growled.

The man registered no outward reaction. He continued to stare straight ahead, beaded sweat pearled along his hairline, but it could have been the warm night. The guy looked like a seasoned pro.

"There is only one way to live," came the reply.

The code exchanged, Bolan holstered Big Thunder. He tugged open the driver's door.

"Glad you made it, Captain. Slide over, please. I'll take the wheel."

The civvies-clad contact clambered into the passenger seat, not releasing the Uzi submachine gun cradled in his lap, his right finger resting on the trigger below the car's window level.

"My apologies for being late. I was slowed by a Lebanese checkpoint that had gone up since yesterday."

Bolan climbed in, kicked the Fiat to life and pulled a hard U-turn, gunning the vehicle back toward the city.

"Will the checkpoint give us trouble on the way in?"

"There are many ways into Beirut, and I know them all," grunted the Israeli. "We stand a fifty-fifty chance of getting in without trouble. Those are good odds on a night like this."

The guy's rough-hewn features reminded Bolan of someone he knew well. This Mossad man, Chaim Herzl, was a nephew of Yakov Katzenelenbogen, the former Israeli intelligence boss who now headed a covert U.S. antiterrorist combat unit called Phoenix Force, which until recently had been under Bolan's command. Captain Herzl looked like the spitting image of a younger Katz.

The Fiat jolted along with less speed than Bolan would have liked, the single headlight pointing the way past occasional deserted-looking clay houses and nothing else. Scars of mortar shells pockmarked the road and countryside.

The two men encountered no military traffic and none of the sporadic fighting that peppered the night, only a few vehicles and pedestrians heading the other way, refugees from the holocaust. The thunder and lightning of war grew fierce as the Fiat drew closer to the city. Flares arced into the sky and cast night into surreal day two miles ahead.

"It is difficult to believe," commented the Israeli, "that Beirut was not long ago regarded as the Paris of the Mediterranean."

Bolan eyed the night beyond the windshield.

"It looks like Nam."

His review of last-minute intel prior to arriving in Lebanon fired to vivid life as the Fiat rattled along.

Lebanon's latest civil war, a vicious struggle pitting Arab Christians against Druse and Shiite Muslims aided and armed by Syria, raged out of control, threatening the very existence of the Christian president's fragile pro-Western government.

Fighting between the bloodthirsty factions flared all around the city. Supply columns traveling the Beirut-Damascus highway enabled the Druse to move Soviet-made artillery and mortar placements into the Shouf mountains overlooking Beirut. Druse forces pounded Christian positions with artillery and Katyusha rockets. Lebanese army tanks and troops fought Shiite militiamen in the city's suburbs.

The Druse, joined by Syrian-backed Palestinian guerrilla forces, hoped to link up with the Shiite leftists on the outskirts of Beirut in a drive to take over the capital. The objective of this uneasy alliance: to topple the duly-elected government and existing political system at the price of a bloodbath.

Artillery fire had rained down on the city throughout the week, hitting hospitals, forcing schools to close, setting homes ablaze.

As always the civilians, caught in the middle, paid the real, terrible price for conflicting political and religious ideologies run amok. Opposing forces accused each other of conducting massacres.

"Turn right at the next road, coming up beyond those trees," instructed the Israeli with a gesture. "We'll be in the thick of it in another mile. There is a Muslim residential neighborhood beyond this turn. Or there was before the inhabitants fled. Those were probably the last of them we passed back there on the road. The situation now is very fluid, not only with the army and the insurgents, but also bandits. Anyone can get his hands on a grenade launcher and do what he likes with it."

"Then let's cover this fast," growled Bolan without taking his eyes from the night. He approached the turn. "You know why I'm here?"

"Strakhov. That's all I know. Except that my uncle has many connections in Mossad from his days there. That is how you got here. My orders are to obey your orders. I don't even know your name, but I am at your disposal."

"Where is Strakhov right now?"

"I am afraid we don't know that."

"Have you been able to learn why he's here? This is a hot spot for a ranking KGB commander to put in an appearance."

"I'm hoping the informer we're on our way to see will shed more light on the subject," said Herzl. "Her name is Zoraya Khaled." He told Bolan the address of the woman's flat not far from the Avenue des Français in central Beirut.

Bolan committed the address to memory.

"You have no clue as to why Strakhov has set up shop in Beirut?"

Strakhov.

The top priority.

The Executioner had come to Beirut to track down the elusive Soviet terror boss, destroy whatever the cannibal had going for him and terminate the KGB major general once and for all.

"It could be assassination," said the Israeli.

Bolan wheeled the Fiat into the turn.

The Muslim suburb up ahead looked deserted under the flickering illumination from the flares and distant fires.

Bolan could hear the sounds of automatic weapons in the distance from several sources, none aimed at the Fiat.

"The president?"

The Israeli nodded.

"Possibly to assassinate him and replace him with an Arab who is Christian but in fact a dupe of the rivals. As you can see, there is anarchy. A successful revolution? It could backfire. Israel could rush in to assist the Christians—the Maronites. Your country would help. The government would prevail."

"Where is the president now?"

"Safe enough. He is under tight security at the presidential palace in Baabda, just outside Beirut. Now you know all that I know. Probably a great deal more. Zoraya will be able to fill you in, I'm sure. Is there anything else?"

"Yeah, there is, Captain." Bolan's voice warmed. "Good work. Your Uncle Yakov sends his greetings."

Herzl started to grin and say something above the din of warfare around them, but at that instant a piercing whistle needled through the other noise.

"Incoming," Bolan snarled. His right arm propelled Yakov's nephew down roughly but effectively.

"Get ready to move!" Bolan punched off the Fiat's headlight and accelerated, veering.

Too late.

The world exploded in a deafening clap.

The Fiat, escaping a direct hit, caught enough of the blast to be lifted up and over. For several heartbeats, reality existed to Bolan as a tumbling kaleidoscope, crunching car metal and shattering glass.

When the vehicle stopped its roll, Bolan felt relief that his body responded to the mental command ordering it to seek cover well away from the car. He experienced another surge at the sight of his companion scrambling from the opposite side of the Fiat as approaching footfalls came up on them. In the arcing glow of overhead flares, Bolan counted four men, civvies-clad snipers wearing the red armband of the Shiite militia.

Bolan and Herzl sought the cover of darkness and undergrowth beyond the road.

The soldiers approached, laughing among themselves. One of them carried a grenade launcher. They all toted Soviet-made Kalashnikov AK-47 assault rifles.

Then one of them spotted Herzl, who had not sought cover fast enough. The militiamen opened fire on the Israeli.

Bolan saw Herzl dive away from the line of fire an instant before two of the Shiite gunmen opened up on him.

Bolan straightarmed the mighty .44 AutoMag and triggered a couple of hammering rounds that blew apart two gunners' heads, pitching their corpses backward. Then The Executioner tracked on the third sniper, who was bringing up his AK in Bolan's direction.

Bolan's survival instincts flared too late at the rustle of attacking movement from behind. He knew this Beirut hit could end for him before it had even begun. The sniper down below him was in his sights, sure, but The Executioner had been outflanked with no time to turn....

2

A 3-shot stutter erupted from Captain Herzl's Uzi from the shadowy clearing across the road.

Two more Shiite bandits tumbled into death sprawls: the last Muslim fanatic, who was carrying the grenade launcher that blasted the Fiat, and a street fighter coming in behind Bolan, stopped forever by the burst from the Mossad agent.

Bolan and the Israeli joined up moments later to survey the now useless Fiat surrounded by the fresh dead and rapidly widening pools of blood.

"I owe you one, Captain. Let's move out."

They jogged away from the scene, traveling parallel to the road for a while in the direction of the buildings on the outskirts of Beirut, a half mile away.

"This far from the fighting, those men could only have been out for themselves," Herzl opined.

"Kill crazy," snapped Bolan.

There appeared to be a lull in the shelling of the city.

Beirut pulsed with the panic of its civilian population in the fires and devastation that assaulted the senses wherever one looked. Small-arms fire and the grumble of tank fire continued here and there.

A flare arced, partially blotted out by thick clouds of smoke from a fire somewhere nearby, but it cast enough light for Chaim Herzl to openly appraise the American in blacksuit as the two of them jogged along.

"As you can see, my friend, you will not stand out moving through the streets of Beirut tonight in your combat suit and weaponry. Tonight belongs to Death."

They passed a haphazard pile of four entangled bodies. PLO. Ropes had been tied around the dead men's necks, the heads almost torn loose from the bodies.

"Dragged behind trucks," Herzl explained as they continued past. "No one takes prisoners here."

Bolan lifted a hand to silence the Israeli and Herzl got the message.

Both men fell farther away from the road.

An army tank rumbled into sight from behind a row of two-story, battle-scarred buildings. The war machine clanked by, never slowing as it passed the spot where Bolan and the Mossad man took to cover.

"On their way to investigate our firefight," Bolan noted.

"They will find nothing but dead Muslims, which is what they want to find," whispered Herzl. "The Fiat cannot be traced."

"How far are we from Zoraya's apartment?"

"Quite frankly, considering the situation in Beirut tonight, we could probably get there on foot in the same amount of time it would take to drive. There is heavy fighting between here and where she lives."

"All the better to be on foot then," Bolan remarked. He looked in the direction of the Lebanese army tank that had been swallowed by the night. "Let's move out. They'll be back when they find out there's nothing over there to shoot at."

They left their cover and continued on, cutting across an alley.

Automatic weapons stammered in the distance two or three blocks away. Bolan heard people screaming.

"The soldiers are not our main concern," Herzl warned. "The Maronite Phalangist militia...they will shoot at anything that moves."

Bolan knew of the Phalangists, the radical military arm of a powerful political party in Lebanon.

It had been Phalangist militiamen who slaughtered those hundreds of unarmed Palestinian refugees following the assassination of a Lebanese president a couple of years back.

Herzl led Bolan from one deserted back dirt alley to another, moving ever deeper into Beirut, toward the worst of the devastation.

Sporadic gunfire could be heard in the near distance.

Bolan caught vivid glimpses of pure havoc each time he and the Israeli darted across a side street that bisected the alleys.

Everywhere he looked, Bolan saw chaos: walls of buildings disintegrating from the shelling; families, residents standing around numb with shock; automobiles flaming, trashed in the streets; dead bodies sprawled everywhere—Muslim and Christian soldiers and civilians, men, women and children fallen in awkward positions on the sidewalks, in the gutters.

A pack of drunk Phalangist troops were too busy

looting a Muslim store to see Bolan and Herzl slide by behind them. The cries of the wounded and others mourning their dead echoed throughout the ravaged city.

I have arrived in Hell, Bolan thought.

The farther they penetrated via the network of alleys, the worse it became.

A frightened family rushed past them on foot, heading in the opposite direction. The father watched the two armed men dash by and muttered a warning in Arabic that Bolan could not understand. Then Bolan and the Israeli passed the family, cutting toward another side street.

"He says we are crazy," Herzl explained, "and perhaps he is right. But our luck is holding out."

At that moment they left the cover of the alley in a beeline through the darkness toward an opposite alley that bisected the first block. They were in a neighborhood of Beirut's distinctive multileveled limestone housing projects, many punctured here and there by gaping holes from the artillery bombardment.

Bolan and the Israeli each scanned a different direction up the side street before leaving cover of the alley, as they had done at each cross street during their penetration of the war zone.

The street looked empty enough. Two bodies of dead soldiers were sprawled down the way—nothing more.

The Executioner and Herzl hotfooted across that street and were caught in the open by the abrupt tramp of dozens of running feet from one end of the block as a group of men in the garb of Druse militia charged into view.

At the opposite end of the block a jeep screeched to a stop.

Bolan saw a .50-caliber machine gun mounted on a swivel in the rear of the jeep, manned by a bearded Phalangist soldier.

Bolan and Herzl readied themselves as they ran for the safety of the mouth of the alley across the street.

Bolan thought they would make it.

Then he caught movement several feet away and a small shadow took form.

"A child," Bolan grunted.

He dived toward a little five-year-old in rags who had somehow wandered from nowhere into this killground. Bolan reached the dirt-smudged bundle and fell across the child as a human shield.

The machine gunner in the jeep opened fire on the Druse in the street. The heavy reports hammered Bolan's eardrums and almost smothered the screams and shouts of the dying as .50-caliber slugs leveled the Muslim militiamen like a scythe chopping wheat. The bullets zinged well over Bolan and the child he protected.

There was a lull in the firing. The screaming stopped.

Bolan scrambled for the alley, carrying the boy. The Executioner only caught a glimpse of the slaughter splashed across the Beirut street amid a swirling cloud of gunsmoke from the machine gun.

Clutching the Uzi, Herzl stepped out from the shadows to better cover Bolan and the boy.

The Phalangists did not see the big warrior in blacksuit in the gloom. Bolan heard them good-naturedly congratulating themselves.

Then more movement came from the opposite corner of the block. At least a dozen Muslim fighters and other combat uniforms Bolan recognized as PLO charged the Lebanese army jeep, raining fire on the Phalangists as they ran.

Herzl turned to track his Uzi on the new danger when the machine gunner in the jeep opened fire, spraying the alley in a stitching cross fire.

Bolan heard the thwack of bursting flesh and a scream. Instinctively he knew what had happened even before he turned around. Herzl had caught a round in the chest. The nightwarrior continued to shield the kid from gunfire as he watched the Israeli stumble.

Bolan raced to the fallen Israeli and grabbed his shirt collar. The hell-blitzer pulled all three of them—himself, the Mossad man and the Arab child—out of the line of fire.

Herzl collapsed against a wall in the alley. Bolan looked at the guy, whose chest was a bubbling dark horror. Herzl coughed blood and lifted his eyes to Bolan, who crouched beside him, cradling the boy in his left arm. The three figures huddled in the narrow street while the battle raged around them between the crazed factions.

Bolan clenched his teeth in anger as he palmed the AutoMag. A good man lay dying and Bolan could not do a goddamn thing to save him. No one could with a wound like that.

"Y-you will have to carry on alone." The mortally wounded Israeli's voice could barely be heard above the fighting. "Zoraya...trust her...."

Bolan's gut constricted with rage and a pain of regret. He had brought this young man to die out here tonight.

"Chaim, dammit—"

The man on the ground coughed more blood, darker this time, as he struggled to touch Bolan's shoulder.

"You are not to blame...I understand the...importance of your mission.... T-tell my uncle...."

And Chaim Herzl died.

The fighting in the street became more intense.

A rush of movement came from the alley entrance a few feet away. A street fighter with PLO insignia, toting a smoking AK-47, charged headlong for the opposite end of the alley to outflank the Phalangists. Then he saw Bolan and the child and the dead man in the shadows. The guerrilla paused in midstride with a grunt of surprise and started to swing the AK in Bolan's direction.

From where he knelt beside the slain Mossad agent, Bolan twisted slightly, not releasing the child, and tracked up the AutoMag to trigger a round.

The PLO killer's skull exploded in a dark cloud and the terrorist reeled backward.

Two Phalangist militiamen appeared in the dimness at the opposite end of the alley. They also had the bright idea of outflanking their enemy. When they detected movement and shooting in the gloom around Bolan, they opened fire immediately with U.S.-supplied M-16 assault rifles.

Bolan propelled himself and his young Arab charge, still clutched tight against his chest, away from the target area. Projectiles razored the space occupied by Bolan only seconds before, the heavy-caliber slugs pulverizing the walls, spraying the alley with a cloud of chips. The lifeless body of Chaim Herzl shuddered from the burst.

Bolan fired two more rounds, evenly spaced, accurate enough to blow away the two Phalangists, who flopped over as if yanked from their feet by invisible wires. These two would massacre no more refugees.

Bolan made a dash for safe ground. He passed the sprawled militiamen and leaned against the wall at a cross street, slamming a fresh clip of 240-grain headbusters into the butt of the AutoMag.

The impressive handgun came as close to a rifle as any handgun could, the ammunition produced by marrying a .44 revolver bullet to a cut-down 7.62mm NATO rifle cartridge case, capable of enough velocity to tear through the solid metal of an automobile-engine block. When the hand cannon roared, the enemy stayed down.

After reloading the AutoMag, Bolan put his arm around the boy once more. He remained remarkably quiet, probably too exhausted, in shock, but now the little guy lifted a smudged face to the man who held him and cried out something plaintive in Arabic.

Bolan knew how the kid felt. He felt like crying out in anguish himself.

The misery had to stop.

Bolan held the future of this country in his arms— part of the future. He hugged the scared little child tighter and murmured comforting sounds, close to the small tousled head, with paternal strength. The child uttered a few more Arabic words and by the gaunt look of his cheeks, Bolan guessed that he was hungry.

Then the little tyke closed his eyes and drifted back into an exhausted half sleep, quiet as could be. Something closed around Bolan's heart as he looked at the kid's troubled features. Even at this tender age the boy knew how to stay the pangs of hunger—sleep.

The nightfighter leaned around the corner of the alley. He saw some activity at the far end of the block, but on this side the night and The Executioner had the street to themselves.

The firefight tapered off in the next street over, the .50-caliber gun silenced. Bolan heard short bursts of small-arms fire every few moments, then nothing from that direction. He took a deep breath, the acrid smell of gun smoke stinging his nostrils.

Diplomacy had obviously failed in Lebanon. Too many had suffered for too long: innocents like the homeless waif that Bolan rescued; Arab Christian and Muslim alike, exploited by power brokers who sacrificed the lives of others for their own obsessive greed; and now his friend Yakov joined the ranks of the suffering, bereaved of his nephew. It had to stop.

The next generation, the real future of this troubled land, must have the opportunity to grow in a stable society, free of the threat of war. Then, perhaps, the population could strive to reach full potential instead of slaughtering each other until the gaps of hate and difference become unbreachable. Direct, positive action could do it, applied with proper control and audacity.

Bolan-style.

The Executioner knew that his present was immutably severed from his past. And although, in blessed moments, his life touched those of his fearless friends—the men of Phoenix and Able, Grimaldi, Turrin, Kurtzman and those lovely women, Smiley, Toby and their associates—his future was committed to acting under his own command. He was answerable to no one and to nothing except his understanding, born in flames, of justice. There would always be room in his campaign, of course, for his allies.

Dire events had conspired once more—relentlessly and inevitably, it now seemed to Bolan—to impel him onto this lonely odyssey. Bereft of his legions, he accepted his due stoically, determined to pursue his destiny to the end. He knew this war was really his and his alone. Why? Because his war was a simple matter: he would avenge to the last drop of blood the death of April Rose.

In the States, Yakov Katzenelenbogen routinely received intel reports from the Mideast, considered of possible interest to his erstwhile commander by contacts Katz maintained in Mossad.

When the Phoenix Force boss received news that Greb Strakhov was in Beirut, Katz immediately processed the item to Bolan via one of their standard floating contacts maintained since Bolan went "outlaw."

Bolan had agreed: they could not afford to let such an opportunity pass to strike at the top-echelon member of the Soviet terror machine, the man at the head of those who had killed his beloved April.

Katz covered Bolan's travel to the Mideast under anonymous Israeli diplomatic immunity. Bolan's weapons and munitions had been shipped by air, hidden in crates of Tel Aviv-bound machine parts, with

Mossad's Security Blue authorization, which meant no one checked them.

In Israel, Bolan had retrieved his hardware without any problems—there are no gun-control laws in Israel—and Katz had accompanied the Executioner as far as the Lebanese border. There, an Israeli military patrol took "the mystery man from the States" into the war-torn Lebanese countryside for Bolan's rendezvous with Chaim Herzl, Katz's nephew.

At that moment, at a military airfield near the Israeli port of Acre, Katz was waiting for word from Bolan or Herzl on the mission.

Bolan did not look forward to telling Katz of his nephew's fate.

Bolan gripped the Lebanese child to his left side, Big Thunder in his right fist, fanning the night, ready to kill. With no more than a whisper, the nightscorcher in black and his human bundle moved deeper into a city that pulsed like something about to explode, taking everything and everyone with it.

He would find two people amid this rubble of war.

Strakhov.

And the woman, Zoraya.

The Executioner had come to Beirut.

And he would give new meaning to the word Death.

3

Bolan had long ago accepted that his was a life destined to be War Everlasting.

In a very real sense, that is the lot of all civilized human beings. Life is a war of ideas, ideologies and actions, the conflict drawing the line between good and evil within ourselves and the society in which we live.

The difference is that Mack Bolan is a soldier, and as such he puts himself on the front lines, where wars are stark and real and lives are lost in the conflict.

It had been a long walk through such hellfire without letup since the days when a young infantryman from Pittsfield, Massachusetts, found himself dubbed The Executioner for his successful sniper missions behind enemy lines during the Vietnam War. The fact that Bolan was also nicknamed Sergeant Mercy for his compassionate treatment of Vietnamese civilians often escaped media mention and still does.

Bolan's life altered dramatically when he received an emergency leave to return home to bury his parents and sister, victims of Mafia violence.

Worthwhile as he considered his work in Nam, the jungle-war specialist made a gut-wrenching decision, considering his military background and dedication to selfless duty. Bolan gave everything he had to anything he undertook. He was more than a good soldier. His record attests to the fact that in his sniper penetration missions, Bolan was the best. No one could match him in tracking, identifying and terminating his target.

But neither was Bolan a man who could bury his family, then turn and walk away when the killers and their employers roamed free. Other good men would carry on his work in the jungles of Nam.

The Executioner could not return to the other side of the world while an all-powerful evil cancer claimed his family and festered from within at the vitals of his country. Bolan did consider himself a patriot, and he was much too American to turn his back on a threat like that.

The Army-trained Executioner declared a wholly illegal war against the Mafia. Bolan used all his Special Forces training in a war of attrition to keep the cannibals at bay before it was too late.

At first Bolan was consumed by thoughts of vengeance. But he quickly realized the danger inherent in such an attitude. So he reassessed his feelings carefully, discovering that he could provide the hard edge between the civilized and the animals in the street. Bolan saw no justice in the halls of justice, so he personally delivered the tab to Mafia slimeballs for their lifetimes of sin.

Bolan accomplished the impossible.

The Executioner brought the vile behemoth to its knees in thirty-eight audacious campaigns, in the process doing what law-enforcement agencies had been unable to do.

This led to a top-secret government pardon with Bolan "dying" and being reborn with a new identity—Colonel John Phoenix, head of America's covert antiterrorist wars.

The enemy had not changed, as far as Bolan, or Phoenix, was concerned. The terrorist network tried to do to the world what the Mob had tried with a country.

Now, though, Mack Bolan was on the run.

A lone outsider waging a solo war for justice in a hostile world.

After twenty-four successful antiterrorist missions, Bolan witnessed the slaying of the woman he loved during an assault on his command center. He found and terminated the KGB mole, planted at White House level, responsible for planning the attack. Bolan canceled the Russian ploy to sabotage America's intel apparatus from within. But an unavoidable result was the blowing of the elaborate cover of John Phoenix and his government-sanctioned missions with his combat units, Phoenix Force and Able Team.

The public, the Mafia, the KGB—the world—now knew that Mack Bolan, The Executioner, was alive.

Especially the KGB.

The death of April Rose was permanently seared on Bolan's soul. April died stopping a bullet meant for Bolan. He owed it to her to keep on.

He owed it to himself.

But Bolan could never again "come in from the cold" as he had during his Phoenix period.

Phoenix Force and Able Team continued to play vital parts in America's antiterrorist operations, but

Bolan preferred not to complicate the lives of his buddies by contacting them.

His past was now wired by the CIA, FBI, NSA—the whole acronymic litany of intelligence agencies around the world. Those groups feared the lone warrior to be a security risk because of his unsanctioned activity.

The orders to all agents in the field: Terminate Bolan with extreme prejudice.

The Executioner had shifted operations to a new target: the Soviet spy-terror network, the KGB. The real force behind the action that killed April Rose.

Same breed as the Mafia, sure.

Cannibals that had to be stopped.

Bolan's Phoenix period made him realize that in centering his efforts on individual acts of world terrorism, he had concentrated on tentacles, not the heart of the beast. The principal enemy was a force of seven hundred thousand agents worldwide, specializing in subversion, oppression and terror. Its aim: world domination. Its name: the KGB.

Bolan knew from hard-fact intel that everything from the attempted assassination of the Pope to international debate over cruise missiles could be traced to the headquarters of the KGB's First Chief Directorate in Moscow.

Just as he understood during his Mafia wars that the majority of Italians had nothing but hatred toward the Brotherhood, Bolan understood, too, that the Russian people and the general civilian populace under dictatorial rule in Soviet-occupied countries were not always to be confused with their oppressors.

Major General Greb Strakhov was the main focus of Bolan's KGB war.

Strakhov. The KGB's most powerful official.

Bolan had killed Strakhov's only child, his son, Kyril, during the Executioner's mission to steal a Russian superhelicopter in Afghanistan. Ridding the world of Bolan became an obsession with Strakhov.

War Everlasting for Mack Bolan, right.

And the citizens of Beirut had it no better.

THE EXECUTIONER TRACKED deeper into the horror, traversing battle-ruined neighborhoods barely controlled by rival militias and roving bands of gunmen.

Bolan knew from experience that urban warfare is the soldier's most dangerous hellground. The fields of fire were restricted, clearly limited by walls, sharp architectural lines making hidden observation difficult and stretches of consistent color making undetected movement hard, even for a hellgrounder of Bolan's savvy and expertise. And there was the ever present danger from unlimited positions above—each street a killground deathtrap.

The city was a no-man's-land of jittery shooting, explosions in the night, smoke and licking tongues of flame.

A frightened city under siege.

Bolan kept to dark streets and alleys with the little Arab kid he toted.

The nightrunner avoided the presence of battling factions during his hazardous penetration. He passed some civilians, but they hurried on with eyes averted from yet another man with a gun in the city of death.

The shelling from the mountains had not resumed, for which Bolan was thankful.

He had no time to slow down for news of the fighting or to contact Yakov across the border.

He crouched in deepest shadow in the rubble of a bombed-out store and let trained patience take over as he made a careful scan of the run-down apartment building where Chaim Herzl had told Bolan he would find the Arab informant.

The nightprober eyed the area, his gaze encompassing the entire scene, watching for movement out of his peripheral vision.

He detected no military or armed presence in or around the building.

He unleathered Big Thunder again, lugging the child as he broke cover in a silent dash forward. He avoided the front entrance of the building, cutting to an alleyway midway up the block. He approached a flimsy back door, found it locked and kicked his way on through with a minimum of sound.

No one in sight.

He moved up rubble-littered steps to the second-floor landing and slowed his approach, sacrificing speed for stealth. He hugged the graffiti-covered walls where the rotted floorboards would not creak, using a toe to clear the rubble of shattered glass and broken brick and mortar in his way.

He heard a rattle of gunfire in the night a few blocks away, then the rumble of a tank, its throaty blast fiercer than the others.

Inside the building, nothing but a tomblike silence.

And quivers of danger from all around.

There would be no sanctuary from the hell storming Beirut tonight.

Not that Bolan wanted any.

He would play this one on the heartbeat. There could be room for planning when he had more to work with, but right now all he had was a target.

Strakhov.

For The Executioner, that was enough.

4

A low-watt bulb barely illuminated the second-floor corridor.

Bolan made his way to the apartment specified by Chaim Herzl and tapped lightly on the door with the barrel of the AutoMag. Then he stepped well back from the line of possible fire, pressing himself against the wall of the corridor, AutoMag up, ready to kill. He glanced at the boy still slumbering away in his arms. Keep it up, kid, he thought. He had to be ready to move if. . . .

The door creaked inward a few inches.

An Arab woman stood there, a dusky, dark-tressed beauty dressed in a traditional floor-length caftan that did nothing to conceal a well-shaped figure.

She saw Bolan and started to speak in Arabic.

Bolan stopped her with a motion.

She stepped aside. He carried the boy into the apartment. She closed the door and turned to lean against it, studying the man and child with expressive, inquisitive eyes.

"Do you speak English?" Bolan asked.

"You are from Chaim?"

"Are you Zoraya?"

"Yes. Who are you, please?"

"I'd like to see some identification."

The beauty flared.

"You dare to demand identification from me in my own home?"

Then her eyes softened with concern as she seemed to set aside business for the moment. She stepped forward, instinctively it seemed to Bolan, and plucked the child from Bolan's grasp. "And who is this?" she asked Bolan.

The child and the woman considered each other for a few moments, and some of the distrust ebbed from the little guy's big eyes.

"He needs shelter," Bolan growled. "I don't know what happened to his parents. We've been through a lot getting here."

"He is hungry. He must be fed."

The woman turned with the boy and walked into a kitchenette. The apartment contrasted sharply to the rest of the rubble-strewn building complex. The lady kept her home neat and clean, with Spartan furnishings.

Bolan did not holster Big Thunder. He cautiously checked the bathroom and bedroom while the woman prepared food for the child. Then Bolan holstered the AutoMag. He crossed to a window, noting the apartment was sensibly lighted by a floor lamp that was across the living room from the window.

He parted the draperies a fraction of an inch and glanced up and down the street below Zoraya's window. A camouflage-painted truck with a rocket launcher mounted behind turned the corner past the flames of a trashed car, redeploying to some new position. The fighting would resume. The city trembled with expectation of the violence everyone knew had to come.

While the boy sat on a divan and ate, the woman stepped up to Bolan, extending Lebanese photo ID for his inspection. The ID backed up her claim that this was her place.

Bolan accepted that.

For now.

"Captain Herzl gave me your address. What do you know about Major General Strakhov?"

He sensed a sharp mind weighing it all behind deep eyes that dominated a high-cheekboned face.

"How...do I know I can trust you?" she asked. "Chaim was to come here tonight."

"Chaim is dead."

Bolan expected her reaction. He had not missed her reference to the Israeli agent by his first name.

She took it like a bayonet in the gut, a gasp of shock. Bolan could tell by the fleeting look of pain on her face that part of the mind wanted to reject what it heard even as the hurt exploded through her. Then she pulled herself together in a visible effort, holding in everything that wanted to burst out.

"We were lovers," she told Bolan. Her voice quavered.

"I understand. I'm sorry."

Bolan told her how Chaim died trying to cover Bolan as he rescued the boy.

"It...was an honorable way to die," Zoraya said softly when she heard it all. "I am no stranger to death."

"I'm moving fast," he told her. "You've got to tell me. Chaim said you knew something about why Strakhov is in Beirut."

"Strakhov. We will all die because of him."

"Why were you informing to Chaim?" Bolan asked. "Because you loved him?"

"Not at first. Love...came later. I had two brothers. I am Druse. I can see by your eyes that you did not know this. My brothers volunteered for the militia to fight the Israelis and the Lebanese army. Do you know the injustices we Druse have suffered at the hands of this government, and yours?"

"And yet you inform for Mossad. You fell in love with one of their agents."

"Aziz and Adli were slain not by the Israelis or the army," the woman told him. "A Maronite spy was discovered in the squad in which my brothers fought. My brothers' officers suspected someone in the squad had arranged it. A ridiculous charge. My brothers were devout servants of Allah and the Druse cause. They were summarily executed, as were the others in the squad.

"At first, I informed out of anger. Then I began to understand Chaim and what he believed. I understood there were other ways to bring peace. I do not inform to hinder the Druse cause, but to further it. I have never passed information that would result in the wholesale death of my people. I only want to help diffuse this tension. Chaim understood."

"I understand, too. But from what I've seen tonight, Zoraya, you're not doing too well."

"There is no hope," she said with quiet desperation. "Chaim is dead. The dogs of war run wild."

"Strakhov," Bolan prodded gently. "What have you learned about him?"

"Yes, of course. I'm sorry. It is something very high level. Security makes it all very vague. The major general is billeted with the Syrian army at Zahle, less than thirty miles from here. This knowledge in itself is enough to get one killed."

"Chaim mentioned an assassination."

"He told you that? I had not made the connection."

"Zoraya, if it's supposed to happen tonight, perhaps I can stop it."

"I know none of the details. It has all come to me in a very roundabout way, you understand. Something overheard in a crowd, repeated many times before it reached me. You know of the Disciples of Allah?"

"Shiite fanatics," Bolan growled. "Broke off from the militia because the Amal weren't killing Christians fast enough."

The Disciples had been one of two Shiite groups to claim responsibility for the truck-bomb massacre of U.S. Marines at the airport.

"The Disciples of Allah operate from Biskinta, about twenty miles northeast of Beirut," said Zoraya.

Bolan recalled intel from his briefing by an Israeli army officer at the airfield across the border five hours before Bolan penetrated Lebanon.

"Biskinta. The Iranians control that area."

Zoraya nodded.

"The Iranian Revolutionary Guards. Volunteers in the war against Israel. The Iranians are sworn to fight and die for their oppressed Shiite brethren around the world. Fanatics, yes. The Iranians supplied the Disciples with the explosives that killed your Marines.''

The little Arab boy had finished wolfing down his meal.

Bolan crossed the room for another look out the window while Zoraya got a blanket from a closet and wrapped the child in it.

Nothing moved in the darkness of the street.

Bolan heard Zoraya ask the boy some questions in Arabic in a tender, motherly tone, but the little guy's eyelids drooped shut before his tousled head touched the arm of the couch.

Zoraya returned to the man in the blacksuit.

"I fear our little one is still too afraid to speak. I cannot get him to tell me his name. But he should sleep for hours.''

"Thanks for your help.''

"I could not do otherwise. But now... there is your mission.''

Bolan found himself pacing, itching for action.

"I've got Shiite fanatics, Biskìnta and an assassination. What else, Zoraya? Whose assassination? The president of Lebanon?''

"I do not know. I am sorry.''

The warrior forced himself to stop pacing. He thought aloud, trying pieces of the puzzle for size.

"I can see why you didn't make a connection between Strakhov and the Disciples of Allah or the Revolutionary Guards. The Russians and the Iranians don't get along. But something big could change that. A common interest. An assassination. You said Strakhov is at Zahle now with the Syrians?''

"Yes, the major general left the base early this evening with a detachment of Syrian troops. My contact in Zahle is my sister, who cooks for the Syrians."

"It's happening tonight," Bolan decided, "and Strakhov has to be tied in one way or another, whatever it is. I've got to get to Biskinta. I'll need transportation. Can you help me again?"

"I have a car. May I come with you? I do not want to be like my neighbors, hiding with the lights off, waiting to die. I must be doing something. I know the way to Biskinta. I can drive."

"You're on," Bolan returned, and he looked at the sleeping child on the couch. "Is there a hospital on the way?"

"No, but it would not matter if there were. The hospitals, those that have not been destroyed...their personnel work around the clock. No one would have time to take in another lost soul."

"Then he's safer with us. Okay, lady. Let's take that drive."

She gathered car keys, tossed them into a purse and Bolan saw a 9mm Browning Hi-Power before she snapped the purse shut. Then she gently picked up the blanket-wrapped bundle without waking the little boy.

Bolan motioned her to the side when they were ready to leave her apartment. He flicked off the light switch, drew the AutoMag and prepared to open the door a crack to check the hallway before they left.

Zoraya touched him on the arm in the darkness before he unlatched the door, her fingertips graceful, transmitting deep emotion.

"May I know your name?"

"Does it matter?"

"To me, yes."

He told her.

She repeated it in the stillness.

"Mack. It is a strong name. I know much about you, you see, from the short time we have spent together. You use your strength to build a better world, not to tear it down in ruin as those all about us tonight would. Chaim was like that. I could not bear to think of two such men dying in one night. Promise me, Mack...do not risk your life for me. Please."

He unlatched the door, pulled it inward a crack and peered out.

No one lurked in the hallway.

"Let's go!" said the Executioner.

The mission.

Strakhov.

And one word: assassination.

And a war about to blow wide open again at any second, engulfing them all.

5

They traveled a circuitous route out of Beirut. Bolan's blacksuit, weapons and gear were hidden beneath a blanket that covered him to the neck. Zoraya steered her Volvo through the labyrinth of streets she knew so well. The Arab child snoozed in the back seat as the Volvo bumped along the crater-scarred road.

Bolan wished he could fully trust this woman.

Chaim had vouched for her, sure. Bolan had seen her ID, right. But The Executioner had kept breathing all these years, all these miles through blood, by not taking one damn thing as it appeared.

Especially in the heat of battle in a hostile, alien environment.

Especially not on a night like tonight.

The damn thing was, Bolan liked the human being who said she was Zoraya.

She had not faked the humane instinct that transformed the tough, gun-packing Zoraya to gentle protector of the Arab waif.

With the shelling of the city temporarily ceased, the streets funneled a surge of pedestrian and vehicular traffic trying to get out despite the pre-dawn hour. The mass exodus only served to blur already tenuous lines between Muslim and Lebanese Christian forces. Lines that were impossible for even the militias themselves to determine.

No one slept in the war zone tonight.

The woman drove them from the city along the coast. A sea breeze cooled the air.

The war seemed not so immediate out here.

They passed djellaba-robed Muslims standing before their homes, observing the noises of war from the direction of the city, ruminating camels tethered to trees.

Both sides of this stretch of the main road were littered with debris: the charred remains of trucks, tanks and human corpses.

Two miles north of Beirut, Zoraya turned onto a secondary road, taking them northeast.

"This leads to Biskinta."

"We've been damn lucky," Bolan noted, never taking his eyes from surveying the dangerous night.

"Twenty-four hours ago, we would not have gotten this far," Zoraya said. "Militia checkpoints were everywhere. But the new fighting has changed everything. The armies are busy with each other."

As she spoke those words, the Volvo rounded a bend and Bolan saw the lights of a military checkpoint blockading the road a quarter of a mile ahead.

He positioned himself sideways in the seat, like a man taking a rest. He made a final check to ensure the blacksuit and drawn Beretta were fully concealed. Zoraya slowed the Volvo as they approached the lights.

"The instant it goes wrong," he told her, "get us out of here."

The lady looked tough enough and competent behind the wheel.

Bolan kept his finger ready on the silenced 93-R's trigger beneath the blanket.

Zoraya braked to a stop at the checkpoint. A guard shack stood to one side and next to it three men, wearing the informal Druse militiaman's uniform of parka, knit hat, jeans and combat boots.

The three were armed with Russian AK-47 assault rifles.

Another soldier stood beside a jeep, near a radio in case anything went wrong.

Tension crackled in the night as one of the soldiers approached the car. The others stood behind him, their AKs leveled.

Bolan feigned sleep.

The Arab beauty would handle the soldier.

Bolan could not understand the dialogue, but the exchange did not need translation. He had briefed Zoraya on what to say.

She showed her papers to the militiaman.

"This is my husband and child. My husband was wounded in the fighting. We have been to the hospital in Beirut but had to leave after his surgery to make room for more wounded. He is heavily sedated, as you can see. We are Druse. We live in Biskinta."

"You are crazy to return," the soldier said gruffly, returning the ID with barely a glance at Bolan or the child. "The fighting in the hills is bad. You should not go back."

"It is our home. We return to get our belongings."

At that moment, the little boy in the back seat let

out a caterwaul that echoed off eardrums and did not stop.

Zoraya played it to the hilt.

"There, you see?" she bitched. "My child is awake. Do you want to nurse him back to sleep?"

The soldier grunted something and stepped back from the car and waved her on through, already half forgetting the refugees and, like his companions, warily scanning the barren darkness around them for the enemy.

Bolan reached for the child, who continued to raise a hellish racket. He tried rocking the kid, making clucking noises that did no good. He became aware of a quiet chuckle from the woman behind the wheel.

"Perhaps we should trade places," Zoraya suggested.

When they made the first dip in the terrain that put them beyond sight of the checkpoint, she steered onto the shoulder.

Zoraya took the little one and when the kid's scared eyes saw her, the squawling diminished to a murmur.

By the time Bolan got behind the wheel, Zoraya had the boy in her lap in the passenger seat, the boy transformed once again into a purring angel.

Bolan allowed a chuckle of his own as he steered the Volvo back onto the road.

"Thanks again."

Bolan went back to scanning the night beyond the cone of headlights.

They passed a caravan of four civilian vehicles traveling in the other direction, huddling together for mutual protection.

Zoraya watched the darkness, too, and began crooning soft, soothing tones in Arabic to the child again.

Bolan noticed that the terrain began to incline from the coastal flat into the harsh, rocky foothills of the Shouf mountains.

They would soon be surrounded by Druse artillery, quiet for now, allowing civilian refugees to haunt the roads until the next barrage upon the city. The Druse militiamen did not want to betray their positions to possible retaliatory air strikes.

The mess in Lebanon ranked in a class of its own, but the issues were simple enough.

The mess resulted from so many disparate Muslim factions forgetting their grievances and cross-purposes with each other and uniting—with considerable aid from the Soviet Union—under the banner of Islam in nothing less than a Jihad, a Holy War, against an opposing alliance of similarly disparate factions, in most cases pro-Western.

Bolan knew some history of the region.

In the eleventh century, a group of nonconformist Muslims infiltrated southern Lebanon, eventually coalescing into the Druse community. Unrest between Muslims and Arab Christians dated to the nineteenth century. Druse opposition to Christians was directed particularly against the Maronites, culminating in a series of bloody attacks. After a massacre of twenty-five hundred Christians in 1860, France intervened and the Ottoman sultan was forced to appoint a Christian government, which still was in power.

The current trouble exploded when Israel's military

invaded Lebanon to destroy once and for all the Palestine Liberation Organization. The Israelis succeeded only in driving out moderate PLO factions while diehard PLO terrorists strengthened themselves in an alliance with the Druse.

Druse and PLO fighters operated jointly against the pro-Israeli, pro-Western Lebanese government, joined by the Iranian crazies and the Syrians, in open civil war. Both sides were driven by real grievances, feeding a bloodlust as exploitable as ever by the cannibals who sat on the sidelines and pulled the strings.

Syria, on Lebanon's border, backed the rebel factions in a bid to subordinate Lebanon without necessarily annexing it.

Syria functioned as the Soviets' muscle in this struggle, though Soviet and Syrian interests were often at odds. The Kremlin preferred its clients to remain relatively weak and thus dependent on Moscow's patronage, but the will of Islam is strong. The Soviet terror machine's strongarms in the Mediterranean would never yield to state over religion, the basic tenet of communism to control the masses.

The Syrian warlords in Damascus played the situation with a hope of making Syria the center of the Arab world. Real power, yeah, but not an easy task for a country with nearly no oil and only ten million people.

Damascus already had the PLO under its thumb. Control over the terrorist network gave Syria sinister leverage over moderate pro-Western oil producers who were exceedingly vulnerable to terrorism.

The Russian "advisors," of course, played for the

big stakes. They wanted this corner of the world—a
key to the world slave state their leaders had always envisioned.

The Executioner had a shot tonight at cutting these
savages off at the knees.

But first he had to find Strakhov.

Why had the KGB top cannibal risked it all to come
to this hellground?

Did the answer wait in Biskinta?

Only one thing for sure, thought Bolan. The Disciples of Allah are next.

The slimebags who sent a truck bomb to massacre
sleeping peacekeepers.

Bolan kept his combat-cool objectivity intact as he
drove, but anger tightened his fists around the Volvo's
steering wheel until his knuckles shone bone white.

The Disciples of Allah.

Craziest of the crazies, not giving a damn if they
died, as long as they took plenty of the enemy with
them.

The Shiite fanatics were the most dangerous foe of
all on the battlefield, because they believed they had
nothing to lose.

The desire for martyrdom is rooted deeply in
Shiism, which in turn is rooted in Iran. The very word
assassin comes from *hashshashin* after the gang of
hashish-smoking hit men, directed by an eleventh-
century Persian cannibal named Hasan ibn al-Sabbah,
who often sacrificed their own lives for his cause.

Less than ten percent of the world's five hundred
million Muslims are Shiites, their zeal for martyrdom
fanned by their Ayatollah in Tehran, encouraged by
the mullahs.

During the Iranian revolution, anti-Shah marchers wore white burial clothes to indicate their willingness to die for the struggle. Thousands of Iranian youths wearing red "martyr" bandannas and small "keys to heaven" around their necks volunteered for certain death in the Iran-Iraq war. Children as young as six had been sent to the front with Korans in their hands to clear minefields for the Iranian army.

To die in a Jihad offers a direct passport to Allah and Ali, the revered son-in-law and cousin of the prophet Mohammed.

To kill large numbers of infidels in the process is only a greater glory.

Some enemies, yeah, for one warrior to take on, but Bolan saw no other way.

Some enemies are worth following into Hell.

The Executioner would find Strakhov.

Tonight.

Assassination.

Bolan would find the truth and destroy whatever the KGB terror merchant hoped to feed on from the suffering of this war-torn land.

He glanced sideways and saw the little Arab boy again asleep in Zoraya's embrace.

"Anything?"

"Our little one's name is Selim. I do not think he knows where his parents are, if they are alive or dead. It is all too much for him to comprehend."

Bolan grunted.

"I know how he feels."

"We must do everything we can to find his people when we return to Beirut," said Zoraya, "unless it is already too late."

And a tear the size of a pearl appeared in the corner of one eye and rolled down her cheek. There were no more tears. But Bolan knew they were there inside for the man she had loved and lost to war and for the child in her arms. And if she felt anything like the icy-eyed warrior beside her, she shed a tear for the awful dark side of human beings.

"How far to the town?" Bolan asked, to change the tone and keep the lady tough.

They had driven for ten minutes since the checkpoint, climbing steadily as the road twisted into the hills.

"Very soon," Zoraya replied. "In the next quarter mile there is a trail. It will take you to a promontory overlooking Biskinta."

That suited Bolan just fine.

It was time for action.

Time for The Executioner to strike.

6

The provincial village was tiered across the slope of a mountain. The cluster of look-alike one-story structures was interrupted only by a minaret towering from the mosque from which the muezzins would call the villagers to prayer. The settlement nestled beneath the starlit bowl of the purple sky did not stir.

At the southwestern edge of town was the barbed-wire-enclosed force of the Iranian Revolutionary Guards.

From his position 250 yards to the high ground from the eight-foot-high fence, Bolan could observe, with little chance of detection, the base where the Iranians hosted the Disciples of Allah.

Before moving this close, the nightpenetrator had ascertained that the detachment of Iranians had no roving guard patrols beyond their perimeter.

The base was a rectangle, 250 yards by 200 yards. A heavily guarded gate at the far corner of the compound from where Bolan sat appeared to be the only road in.

The perimeter was well patrolled on the inside by three-man units toting assault rifles.

A row of tents had to be the troops' sleeping quarters, mess and latrines. The big shots could only be quartered and operating out of the squat two-story building in the center of the compound.

The Executioner knew that was where he would find the suicide commandos.

He made a final check of his gear and weapons. He had applied a black facial goo that completed the blacksuit effect, making The Executioner all but invisible this moonless night.

Time: 0300 hours.

Bolan moved out, negotiating the descending terrain in a zigzag course from gnarled tree trunks to inky shadows of wild vegetation.

Zoraya waited with Selim in the Volvo, parked hidden from sight of the main road a quarter mile behind Bolan.

The lady hellgrounder had wanted to accompany him.

"I may be of assistance if you are stopped and questioned," she had reasoned in a low whisper before they parted.

"If I'm stopped, I'll be dead," Bolan had whispered back.

According to Zoraya's intel, Strakhov was on the prowl tonight with an armored Syrian force, and Bolan had little doubt they were in the area, possibly waiting for him with the Iranians at the base.

He would find out.

Alone.

"But I feel so helpless with nothing to do but wait," Zoraya had pressed. "If I am doing something, I—I will not dwell on Chaim. . .on the emptiness that tries to consume me."

"Another reason I won't take you along," Bolan had said. "You'd be killed in a firefight tonight, Zoraya. I don't need that kind of help. And there's Selim. That little character is every bit as important as anything I do tonight. We've got to get him home, and safe."

She had considered that with a glance at the soundly sleeping boy in the back seat of the Volvo.

"You're right, of course." She had appraised Bolan with a frankness he found vaguely disconcerting. "I have the feeling you are right about most things. You are. . . a very impressive man, Mack Bolan."

He had started out of the car.

"Thirty minutes," he had reminded her. "Unless you and Selim find yourselves in danger."

"I will not run out on you."

"Don't worry about me. I want the child safe, and you. Promise me, Zoraya. That kid needs us and I'm not going to let him down."

"I understand. I promise. I shall keep the little one safe."

"Then I'm gone."

Zoraya had leaned over before he closed the car door. She touched his arm.

"Remember, Ib Masudi, the commander of the Iranian Guards. . . his cruelty. . . he is feared more than respected by those in his command. Do not give him quarter under any condition. You are one man taking on incredible odds this night."

"That's the one advantage we've got," had been the soldier's grim parting shot.

The Executioner had turned away and disappeared into the gloom.

The nightfighter had not heard the lady's parting shot, whispered soft as a kiss after him.

"May Allah guide you, angel of death. You deliver His vengeance...."

Bolan intended to play this penetration soft until he could isolate the commander, Masudi, and do all the damage possible before pulling out and leaving the Revolutionary Guards in total confusion. He had faith that such a hit by one man against such a sizable force had a damn good chance of succeeding, considering the hour.

He could see lights on in the building, but except for the sentries at the gates and foot patrols along the perimeter, no one stirred at the base. The guards would not be at their best at this hour. And, of course, Bolan had faith in himself.

He had been doing this type of thing for nearly twenty years in one capacity or another from Vietnam to the present. He understood the risks, the vagaries of such an audacious hit at the heart of the enemy. Talk about vagaries: the Disciples of Allah; an Iranian sadist; something about an assassination; and a KGB boss somewhere in the night with an armored column of Syrians.

Nothing could be planned on a hit such as the one Bolan now contemplated.

He clutched the silenced Beretta in his right fist and came in low at the wire fence, crouching to the base of it. He chose the darkest point between two of the nearest spotlights mounted atop a line of poles evenly spaced along the inside of the perimeter.

He tapped the fence lightly, tentatively. It wasn't electrified. Good.

From a pocket of the blacksuit he produced a miniature set of wire cutters made of a special alloy. He snipped a passage through the fence in seconds.

During his recon he had timed the movement of the sentry patrols. He gave himself another ninety seconds to cross to the back wall of the building.

He hustled the distance, taking his biggest chance, but he met no interference. Along the way he skirted a blacktop tarmac crowded with weaponry, armored personnel carriers, tanks, multiple rocket launchers mounted in the beds of camou-striped trucks—Russian hardware shipped from North Korea by way of Syria to Lebanon as "farm implements."

He briefly considered the advisability of planting some plastique amid all this war machinery. But he could not discount the possibility that he might accomplish all he wanted and still withdraw undetected until his work was discovered in the morning. That would be ideal if Strakhov wasn't here and the track led somewhere else.

He almost made the shadows at the back wall of the headquarters building when three bearded soldiers in Iranian Revolutionary Guard uniform of hooded parka, knit hat and camou fatigues stepped from the back door of the building toting assault rifles. The Executioner figured they were sentries on their way to relieve one of the foot patrols.

Bolan saw them well before the Shiite fanatics saw his shadow emerge at them from the night. Then three sets of eyes widened in panicky reaction, and three mouths started to curse or shout something. But before their rifles could swing up, Bolan knelt in a two-handed shooting crouch and the Beretta quietly sneezed its 9mm death buzzers.

The 3-round death burst sent the trio tumbling off their feet, piling lifelessly into one another.

Bolan continued past without slowing, gaining the door the three men had just stepped from. As he opened the door he realized he could save the play if he moved fast enough.

He found himself in a hallway leading to the front foyer of what appeared to have been a private home before the cannibals moved in and commandeered the building from its owners.

An IRG member stepped into the hallway inquiringly, drawn by the sounds of the commotion outside in the early-morning silence.

The soldier met Bolan eye to eye.

Bolan didn't stop for this one, either. His left hand grabbed the guy's throat, and he rammed the man's head backward against the doorframe hard enough to kill him.

The soldier collapsed, blood trickling from his ears and matted hair to the wood behind him.

Bolan extended his right arm through the doorway of the Orderly Room. As he sailed past he drilled two sleepy-eyed soldiers who started to get up but plopped right back down with tunnels cored through their heads.

The Executioner kept moving.

He reached the foyer and started up some stairs he found there.

The lights he'd seen from this house had come from both levels.

He fed a fresh clip into the Beretta, taking the
treaders three at a time.

Survival depended solely on how fast he moved. His
presence had only been detected by those he killed. But
those bodies could be discovered anytime. And the
patrolling sentries would soon begin to worry about
their reliefs' delay.

The hallway on the second level was lined with
closed doors. Through an archway to Bolan's right
dim light filtered into the corridor along with a male
voice chanting something in Arabic.

Bolan approached the archway, pressing himself to
the wall. No one showed his face as Bolan stealthily
breached the distance, the Beretta still in his fist.

The men beyond that passageway must have felt
secure with the guards outside and downstairs in the
Orderly Room. The only way this thing played to Bolan was that something important had to be going
down for 3:30 A.M. activity.

He reached the archway and crouched well below
eye level of anyone in the room around the entrance
frame.

The voice in Arabic took on a cadence like a prayer.

Bolan stole a glance around the edge of the wall. His
trained eye sized it all up with one sweep.

Six men.

Ib Masudi.

The slight stature of the Iranian commander did
nothing to lessen the cruelty that glittered from eyes
like black marbles separated by a hook nose. The
Shiite general was in full IRG uniform.

That made this an official briefing.

The four men across a table from General Masudi were in mufti but wore Disciples of Allah armbands. One of them was an older man with gray in his beard, most likely the Disciples' military liaison. The others were younger, with the wary body language of street fighters. The terrorists and the general all wore holstered pistols.

They had unrolled and were studying large pieces of paper on the low table.

Blueprints.

Bolan took in the sixth man in the room, then the room itself, and he knew he had it.

Prayer rugs on the floor.

The sixth, a white-bearded old man doing the chanting and wearing traditional djellaba, was unarmed and clasped a Koran to his breast as he spoke fervently.

The Disciples of Allah and Masudi listened intently with downcast eyes to their mullah giving the blessing before another suicide squad stole into the night to bring terror.

Not this time.

The Executioner straightened and stepped from concealment into the room, the Beretta tracking on Masudi, who first noticed the grim specter.

The general's expression warned the others and they looked up, too. In the next heartbeat everyone scrambled for weapons, fanning away from each other with a flaring of survival instinct. The mullah faded back into a corner, wishing he could become invisible.

Then an earsplitting explosion from outside disrupted the confrontation. Windows blew inward and the house shuddered to its foundations.

The sounds of gunfire opened up outside before the rumbling of the first explosion ebbed, followed by a cacophony of slaughter that meant only one thing.

The Iranian base had fallen under attack by someone other than The Executioner.

With Bolan caught right in the middle.

7

The action in the room resumed even as flying shards of glass, blown inward from the windows by the first explosion, sliced through the air.

Four Disciples of Allah terrorists.

General Masudi.

And their Executioner.

The old white-bearded mullah crouched in a far corner of the room on the periphery of the action, shielding himself from exploding glass.

The instant before, Bolan's Beretta 93-R had drawn a bead on the bridge of Masudi's hook nose, but with the attack from outside, everything changed.

A sliver of glass gashed a razor-thin furrow above Bolan's brow. It was only a scratch but deep enough for warm blood to trickle into his eye at the moment everything shifted. He did not trigger the Beretta, knowing Masudi had managed to dodge in the time Bolan needed to think and clear his vision.

The sounds of full-scale conflict emanated from all around the house, but Bolan's concentration centered on the crazies in the room.

The Shiite terrorist graybeard ranked with Masudi as an equal threat to Bolan. Graybeard pointed his piece, tracking on Bolan.

Masudi did the same. The three other Disciples of Allah weren't exactly discussing the weather, either.

Bolan dived into a roll away from the archway as gunfire exploded, magnified in the confinement of the room, drowning out the battle roar from outside.

Bolan came out of the roll.

The religion-drugged fanatics were still trying to get a lead on him, firing as they did. But the rounds plinked into the walls and prayer table, missing Bolan.

His first targets had to be Masudi and the graybeard. He shifted the Beretta to his left hand, flicking it to auto and unleathering Big Thunder in one continuous movement, raking death from both hands.

The AutoMag sheared off Graybeard's skull from the eyes up, and below that the head became a beard of flowing red atop a collapsing corpse.

Bolan tried to sight again on Masudi, but the hooknosed general moved deceptively fast, grabbing one of the Shiite terrorists and jerking the Disciple of Allah in front of him for cover.

Masudi scrambled backward like a scurrying spider toward the archway, dragging the startled young terrorist with him.

Bolan triggered a 3-shot stutter from the 93-R. A row of slugs sizzled into the terrorist in front of Masudi and the human shield went from startled to dead. But that did not stop the Iranian officer. He tossed the body aside and disappeared in a rush down the corridor out of sight of Bolan, who still had his hands full.

The two remaining Disciples toting AK-47s separated to opposite sides of the room. Both terrorists opened fire on Bolan, the blazing weapons spitting heavy projectiles at him.

The penetrator in blacksuit hit the floor in a forward sprawl and took both of the creeps out before they could adjust their aim.

The terrorist on the left caught a 3-shot burst of 9mms in the heart area and tumbled over sideways, crushing the prayer table on the way down. The other opened his mouth to yell but a .44-caliber headbuster cored the man's eye socket like hot metal through butter, spraying the wall behind bright crimson.

Bolan thought for an instant that he had finished there and started to get up, when he saw a flurry of movement from a far corner of the room.

The ancient mullah flipped away the folds of his holy robe and lifted a Czech Model 23 submachine gun. He screeched something about Allah and kept on screeching, but the words were drowned out by the chatter of the killer song in his hands. The wily old-timer rode the recoil like a pro, but Bolan had already hit the floor again. A pulverizing volley of screaming lead tattooed the wall where The Executioner had been only seconds before. Bolan stroked the AutoMag's trigger once more, blowing away the holy man. His prayers were answered, all right. But the wrong people had died.

The combat outside increased in intensity. Screams from the wounded rose above the roar of weapons. Bolan heard more explosions. Another one rocked the building.

He had to get Masudi.

The Iranian commander could be the next link in the

chain leading to Strakhov, though Bolan had a hunch it could be Strakhov's Syrian force attacking the base.

Only seconds had passed since the Iranian general had disappeared around the archway.

Bolan moved over to the mullah's body, reloading and holstering the Beretta and AutoMag. He picked up the mullah's SMG and fished three extra clips from inside the old man's robe.

The Executioner stepped over the corpse and moved toward the hallway. He could hear running footfalls and the clunking of military gear outside this room. He paused at the smashed table where the men had stood when Bolan first appeared.

Bolan stooped without slowing and grabbed the blueprints that had been the obvious subject of this briefing.

A blessing from the mullah before these Disciples of Allah left Biskinta for... what?

The nightwarrior paused and looked around. He spotted the object someone had pushed behind some chairs.

A suitcase.

With a timer attached to it, ready to be set.

He had no time to further consider suitcases with explosives. He had to get Masudi.

He crumpled the blueprints against his chest and stuffed them beneath the blacksuit. Then he grabbed the suitcase in his left hand.

The archway filled with Iranian Revolutionary Guards, three of them toting AKs ready for action. They charged in, but only one man got off a shot that plowed into the ceiling. A burst from the Czech machine gun in Bolan's right fist stuttered like an angry jackhammer, making the IRG invaders perform a death dance like marionettes gone wild in an epileptic puppeteer's hand.

Bolan charged over their bodies after Masudi. All of the activity since the general slipped the scene had taken less than a minute. But Bolan knew his numbers were almost gone if he hoped to nail Masudi for what he knew and still pull out of this action intact.

He fed a fresh clip into the machine gun and peered into the hallway.

No one.

The house seemed deserted.

The battle continued outside the building. A tank rumbled again. Crumbling plaster rained from the ceiling.

Bolan dashed toward the stairs. He thought it was the only route Masudi could have taken unless the Iranian had not left the building at all, which Bolan doubted. He made the landing and started down.

Masudi had looked like a man on the run to save his ass. Sacrificing that terrorist's life to give himself cover proved that. Bolan doubted Masudi would wait around.

The front door of the house was swinging back shut, indicating the general had just gone through.

Bolan hit the bottom step and paused before leaving cover of the doorway for outside.

Three figures charged in through the back door behind Bolan at the other end of the hall downstairs: Syrian uniforms.

The instant they saw him, the trigger-happy Syrians

opened fire on Bolan, their assault rifles on full-auto.

Dodging the onslaught, Bolan shoved the suitcase safely away and aimed the Model 23. Hot lead scorched the air near him, one projectile zinging close enough past Bolan's ear for him to feel the heat.

Then the SMG bucked in his fists, spitting flame and bullets.

The two Syrians in front screamed and jitterbugged under the hail that shredded flesh and sprayed blood onto the third soldier. Panicking, he started to turn and scream even as pursuing slugs pureed his brains from behind. The three dead tumbled into a heap in the back doorway and Bolan returned his attention to the front, hoping he hadn't been diverted long enough for Masudi to escape.

The Executioner crouched back at the doorway, paused to slam another magazine into the Model 23, then peered out at the turmoil.

The presence of the Syrians he'd just killed prepared the nightscorcher for what he saw.

The Iranian base was now brilliantly illuminated by piercing spotlights and headlights of Syrian tanks and personnel carriers that had already penetrated into the center of the compound. Orange-red flames licked the night sky from the area of tents where the main fighting was taking place.

Syrian and Iranian soldiers ran shooting at each other everywhere Bolan looked.

Bolan saw General Masudi.

Six Syrian soldiers stood around the Iranian officer. The soldiers to a man had their rifles aimed at Masudi's head.

The commander of the Iranian Revolutionary Guards stood with head bowed, his hands handcuffed behind his back. His uniform looked scuffed and dirty.

The general and his guards walked toward three men who stood waiting next to a limo that Bolan knew would be armor plated. Syrian army markings designated it a staff car.

Two Iranian regulars wearing only the trousers of their uniforms with civilian tunics came running around the corner of the headquarters building in Bolan's direction, their rifles ready but not ready enough.

The Executioner diverted his attention from Masudi and the others for an instant and triggered a short burst from the Czech Model 23. The volley stitched the two Iranians, stopping them forever.

The fighting had begun to taper off in the compound.

The Iranian Revolutionary Guards who were not strewn in lifeless disarray all over the base could be seen throwing down their weapons, raising arms in surrender to the Syrian troops who closed in.

Not far from the main house, at least forty surrendering Iranians were being herded together by rival cannibals.

Masudi and his guards reached the Syrian staff car.

One of the three men waiting there stepped into the light and Bolan felt a cold fist clench his gut.

The man could be none other than Major General Greb Strakhov of the KGB. In person.

Bolan pedigreed the two with Strakhov as the local operatives of the Glavnoye Razvedyvatelnoye Upravleniye—GRU— the chief intelligence directorate of the Soviet military that shares overseas assignments with the KGB. The other man was a Syrian officer.

Jackpot.

Except that Bolan would have to move damn fast or this jackpot would slip through his fingers.

The Syrian troopers shoved General Masudi into the limo. Strakhov and the other two also climbed into the car.

Bolan turned and darted back down the hallway. He exited the house into the night via the back door, not slowing for the obstacle course of scattered corpses.

As he passed, Bolan snatched the suitcase with the attached timer device he'd left in the hallway. He charged from the house in the direction of the hole in the fence where he'd entered.

He had considered a direct hit on the group by the limo, but it had been too far from the house for accuracy with the machine gun and he still did not have the big picture.

Okay, review time. They were about to whisk Masudi away. Had the Iranian commander set up this hit on his own troops? From what Bolan had seen and heard of Hook Nose, it could go down that way.

Bolan had to determine where Strakhov intended to take Masudi, and *why*. The Executioner had to fit this piece of the puzzle in with the others to make sure their whole scheme collapsed, and not only part of Strakhov's Lebanon scenario. He could hit Strakhov and Masudi now and terminate them, sure, but Bolan knew when the odds were against him. Uh-uh. The way he saw it, any move now would needlessly endanger his life and that definitely did not fit in the picture for the night.

He had to follow that Syrian staff car when it left the base.

The limo could only take one route out of Biskinta and the Iranians' temporary compound to get to the main roads to either Zahle or Beirut: the same road off which Bolan had left Zoraya and little Selim waiting in the concealed Volvo. The chauffeured car with Strakhov and Masudi would have to pass the spot where Bolan had left the Druse woman and the little Arab boy.

He could make the distance to the Volvo on foot if nothing slowed him. Then he could take a chance on following the limo with his lights off.

Bolan was halfway to the fenced perimeter of the compound, angling away from the opposite side of the house from the limo when he heard a shout to halt. It came from the Syrian soldiers herding IRG prisoners near the house.

Bolan paused, set the timer device on the suitcase for five seconds, then heaved the suitcase. Even as the container left his hand, the Executioner put on a burst of speed, continuing his withdrawal.

The terrorist package from the Disciples of Allah zeroed right into that crowd of Iranians, who had protected and supplied terrorists, and anti-American Syrians who thought it fun to shoot down U.S. reconnaissance planes, to kill and capture U.S. pilots.

The incredible blast of the dynamite-loaded suitcase sent shock waves that pushed the warrior along from behind like a huge hot hand. It started drizzling blood and dull thumps sounded in the night as body parts fell all around him.

Something hollow sounding landed in Bolan's path and he jogged past the wide-eyed, openmouthed features of a bearded man's freshly decapitated head.

He reached the fenced perimeter and on through the hole. He almost made the track that led to the car when he heard movement in the darkness to his left, just before the trail began. He swung sideways low and loose, fanning that flank with the machine gun.

In the starlight, combat-honed night vision discerned two crouched figures: disheveled young men in IRG uniforms, their AK assault rifles tossed to the ground. Bolan judged them to be not much past their teens. When the Executioner stopped they shook their heads and waved their hands frantically, beseeching Bolan in a language he did not understand. But he read it clear enough: these two sought refuge there from the slaughter in the camp.

That was okay with Bolan.

The Executioner granted them a "white flag." Sergeant Mercy continued on his withdrawal.

He covered a dozen paces before warning tremors that had never let him down started battling for acknowledgment at the base of his spine.

It only took the teenage soldiers a moment to consider wasting the blacksuiter, to turn their cowardice into heroism for dropping the penetrator.

Before the AK-47s even left the ground Bolan spun, brought up the Model 23 and triggered the SMG.

Nothing happened.

The damn thing had jammed!

The IRG punks tracked on Bolan, who tossed away the useless weapon and dived for cover.

Each soldier got off one round. One projectile splintered the trunk of the tree Bolan dived behind. The other 7.62mm projectile screamed off harmlessly into the night.

Then Big Thunder spoke loud and deadly and both Revolutionary Guards flew backward with faces transformed into smears as black as the night.

"Idiots," Bolan grumbled.

He jogged back onto the trail with one last glance at the Iranian base.

The fighting down there had ceased, all of Masudi's command either dead or captured.

The chauffeur-driven Syrian staff car left the compound, traveling the rutted road leading from Biskinta, and disappeared from Bolan's view around the far side of the mountain.

It would be a matter of three to four minutes before it would pass the point where Bolan had left Zoraya and the child in the hidden Volvo.

Bolan jogged faster, not holstering the AutoMag.

He met no further interference.

Too many people had died already this night—good people like Chaim Herzl and uncounted, anonymous innocents and others caught in the cross fire of rampant savagery—for Bolan to let this vital thread slip through his fingers.

His view of this mission had altered in the hours he'd been in the country. He had originally come with the sole objective of locating and terminating Greb Strakhov. He now realized he could not leave Beirut without doing something decisive to attempt to restore some course of stability in Lebanon.

It could be done. Bolan wasn't sure just how yet. That's why he could not afford to let the staff car escape.

He reached the darkness alongside the road where the Volvo had been parked just as the headlights of the limo pierced the night, Strakhov's driver making good speed despite the road's poor condition.

Bolan crouched.

The headlights missed him as the limo roared past.

The nightfighter glanced around.

Zoraya, the child and the Volvo were gone.

8

The staff car that raced by Bolan's hidden position had company: a camou-painted, tarp-covered two-and-a-half-ton truck with Syrian army markings rumbled along to catch up. Protection.

The troop carrier could not take the battle-rutted road as fast as the limo. Strakhov must be impatient to get Masudi to their destination.

All right.

Another chance.

The staff car disappeared again around another bend of the mountain road.

Bolan approached one of the trees, the shadows of which had hidden the Volvo from view of the road. He willed himself not to worry about Zoraya and Selim. Emotion dulled the combat edge. He reached up on the run and grabbed a sturdy branch well off the ground and hoisted himself up.

The truck upshifted as the road straightened itself out until the next bend. Good, thought Bolan, who was perched on the branch well above the line of headlights or vision from those in the cab of the truck. The noise of the acceleration would cover any noise resulting from what Bolan had in mind.

As the vehicle lumbered by beneath him, he swung

gracefully from the branch to gain a footing on the step under the passenger-side door.

The nightscorcher opened the door so swiftly that the first thing the Syrian soldier riding shotgun knew of it was when Bolan used his left hand to snap him back hard while his combat knife sliced down. A fountain of blood sprayed the interior of the cab and dotted the windshield. Bolan heaved the body into the gloom.

The driver, who broke his concentration from the tortuous mountain road, reacted too late. Bolan killed him and also tossed the body into the darkness.

The slight jar when the steering wheel changed hands went unnoticed by the soldiers jouncing around in the back of the truck. The tumbling bodies were swallowed from view in the vegetation to either side of the road before Bolan's passengers could see them.

He coaxed more power from the heap and that did get curses and shouts from the back, but nothing more. He rounded another turn in the road into a valley, and the taillights of the limo popped into view. And Bolan knew he still had a hold on this tiger of a night.

GENERAL MASUDI tried not to let his fear show. The Iranian Revolutionary Guard commander felt himself shaking, felt shriveled in his uniform. They had not removed his handcuffs.

Masudi rode in one of the pull-down seats in the spacious tonneau of the Syrian staff car.

Three men sat across from him: a broad, bearlike man whom Masudi did not know and who was flanked by two others he recognized: the Syrian officer,

General Abdel, and the GRU pig farmer, Major Kleb, who both had reputations for ambitious brutality.

Masudi eyed the stranger in the middle. Russian, thought the IRG warlord, probably KGB.

Masudi made his appeal in his own language to the Syrian, inwardly cursing the telltale tremor he heard in his own voice.

"Am I to receive no explanation of what has happened, General Abdel? Why were my men attacked? What—"

Abdel leaned forward and punched Masudi in the mouth with enough force to knock the Iranian to the floor of the jouncing car.

Masudi felt shattered teeth gouge flesh from the inside of his mouth.

"You will speak English," the Syrian snarled, "the only language known to all of us."

Masudi spat chips of tooth and struggled with the language he had learned in Iran before the revolution.

"Yes, yes, of course...of course...I only wish to know—"

Masudi saw Kleb glance to the man in the middle. The stranger barely nodded, and the GRU officer glared back at the bleeding Iranian.

"We are the ones to be informed, desert jackal."

"But...I do not understand—"

"Then it will all be made clear to you in Zahle," Kleb intoned with a trace of smugness. He nodded to the Syrian. "Abdel."

"Wait!" screamed Masudi, not believing how terrified he sounded. He had the briefest glimmer of what countless lost souls he had tortured over the years must have felt. He cowered in the corner of the tonneau.

With a snicker, General Abdel pounced, pistol drawn. The Syrian commenced pummeling the handcuffed man about the head, hitting him over and over again until Masudi lost consciousness.

Kleb watched, wishing he could see more in the dark.

Major General Strakhov appeared not to notice the beating. The KGB officer closed his eyes and leaned back against the staff car's plush upholstery. Sighing, he considered the report he must now make to the Kremlin regarding tonight's action.

Moscow would be pleased.

9

The thirty-minute journey to Zahle cut ever deeper into the Druse-held Shouf highlands. The terrain grew bleak, uninhabitable for miles at a time.

Bolan saw no activity amid the occasional clusters of houses they passed as he steered the Syrian deuce-and-a-half behind the taillights of the staff car. The country people had taken cover to await the dawn.

Zahle was cut from an identical mold to Biskinta, perched on the side of another mountain. But the Syrian base on the outskirts of this village showed a marked superiority to what had passed for the Iranian Revolutionary Guards' security.

The Syrians had been in the country considerably longer than the Iranians and it showed in the three layers of concertina-wired perimeter and the heavily sandbagged defenses, permanent barracks and HQ buildings Bolan saw from the high ground as they approached the compound. The base was about four times the size of the one at Biskinta.

Dawn.

An hour away, maybe less.

Not much time, Bolan thought, looking at his watch.

The fighting would resume at dawn. He could feel it. The air crackled with it.

The gates in the fence opened. The captain of the guards saluted as the staff car sailed through without stopping.

Guard patrols and permanent machine-gun nests along the perimeter made the place five times tighter and harder than the one held by those Revolutionary Guard stumblebums, but the gate officer had already turned to step back into the guardhouse when the troop truck followed the limo into the base from fifty yards behind.

No one paid any attention to the indiscernible features of the driver high up in the cab.

Bolan eyeballed as much as he could from behind the wheel as he steered the troop carrier into the center of the compound past a cluster of parked Russian-made T-34 and T-55 tanks and orderly rows of Russian-made Katyusha rockets.

The limo stopped in front of the long, two-story headquarters building.

Bolan braked the vehicle to a halt some distance behind the staff car, directly in front of the end barrack of a row of similar squat structures twenty yards south of the HQ.

He reasoned that the Syrian command would have its own security in the head shed where Strakhov appeared to be taking Masudi. The men in the back of the truck would be weary from the fighting in Biskinta and, Bolan hoped, anxious to grab sack time on their return here. Their presence had only been required on the drive from Biskinta.

The blacksuit hustled away from the truck when it stopped, well before any of the Syrian troops debarked from beneath the tarp. Let them sort out the puzzle of the missing driver and his shotgun rider.

Bolan gained the far side of the headquarters building. He hurried along the back wall to a row of windows, all dark at this hour. He found one left open against the heat of the day, forgotten when the work-day ended. He used both hands to lift the window and it slid up soundlessly. Bolan moved over the sill.

He had been lucky so far not to be spotted by any of the two-man sentry patrols he had seen walking the base. Though what kind of "luck" it was to be inside an enemy camp, about to lose cover of night was debatable....

He found himself in a deserted office. He unleathered the Beretta and padded stealthily between the inky forms of furniture to the door of the room. He turned the door handle and it emitted a soft squeak that sounded deafening to Bolan. He paused, motion-less, but detected no response from the other side. The headquarters building reminded him of a massive tomb. He hoped it wouldn't be his.

The hour: 0410 hours.

Tomorrow would be a big day for the battalions quartered here, if Bolan's gut instincts about this thing were right. The base would be coming to life within the next twenty minutes.

He cracked the office door inward and peered into an unlighted hallway. He heard activity, the sounds of voices in Arabic down at the far end of the building: probably an officer giving orders to the night-duty staff. Then footsteps headed upstairs to the second level of the building, leaving security tight on what they thought to be the only entrance in.

Bolan glanced in the other direction of the corridor and saw another unlighted stairway closer to his position. He moved swiftly, gaining those stairs and starting up without notice of the soldiers in their Orderly Room at the other end of the long corridor. He raced upstairs, the Beretta 93-R on 3-shot mode, ready to spit death. He reached the top landing and looked down this hallway just in time to see a door slam shut. The rest of this level felt more tomblike than downstairs.

The Syrian CO's office would be up here.

That's where they took Masudi.

Bolan expected to find Strakhov here, too.

The target.

The execution.

And the job would be done.

He poised, ready, to make sure no one from below followed the party up here, then he eased around the corner, five quick paces to the door next to the one where they had taken the Iranian.

This door was locked and Bolan extracted a tiny tool from his penetration gear. He was almost through picking the lock when he heard footfalls on the stairs behind him. He finished his illegal entry, then slipped into the room, leaving the door slightly ajar.

A lone Syrian sentry made it to the landing where silent death waited ready for him. The guy didn't hear or see his executioner until this dark apparition confronted him. Before the man had time to react or scream, combat-hardened fingers were slicing the air toward his throat. The punishing thrust ruptured the guy's windpipe, and the man uttered only a muted gurgle before he stopped breathing forever.

Bolan grabbed the sentry before his dead fall could alert those downstairs or beyond the door through which they had taken Masudi. The Executioner hauled the body and rifle over the threshold. Bolan placed the dead man and his rifle on the floor and relocked the door. Then he looked around.

An office.

Chances were good that no one would find this corpse until after it was too late.

Bolan moved to the window.

This side of the HQ building faced away from the barracks.

The first gray smudge of false dawn etched the mountains in the east in stark silhouette.

Bolan moved fast. He unlatched the office window and opened it. A narrow ledge ran beneath the window, around the building. He climbed out onto the lip.

A bloodcurdling scream emanated from behind a lighted window a few feet from Bolan.

He inched forward, pressing himself against the building, never relaxing his sense-probing of the night. He almost reached the window when two sentries strolled shoulder to shoulder around the far corner of the building and approached on a course directly below him.

Standing motionless on the ledge, Bolan did not even breathe, his heart thumping against his rib cage.

One of the sentries glanced up almost casually at the lighted square, the only illumination along the second level of the building. He saw nothing but shadows around the window. He and his companion continued on their rounds.

Bolan heard harsh voices coming from behind the glass. He inched the final distance along the parapet for a glimpse inside the room.

It made sense for Strakhov to bring Masudi here, Bolan mused. The Soviet embassy in Beirut would be buzzing, and for the most part the Soviet terror machine kept a low profile in the Middle East, according to Bolan's considerable intel gained from documents captured during The Executioner's hit in Russia.

The situation in Lebanon was far too fluid, changing minute by minute, for anyone's intel to be very accurate, but the KGB habitually avoided direct active presence here, letting their Syrian clients front for them. Bolan had a suspicion that even the KGB's Beirut control knew nothing of the events at Biskinta tonight, or even of Strakhov's mission to Lebanon. Strakhov's activities since arriving had clandestine written all over them.

Bolan eyeballed the scene through the window.

They had Masudi in the office, sure enough.

Bolan pegged it as the Syrian CO's office.

Masudi sat in a wooden chair, nursing his right hand, rocking back and forth. His handcuffs had been removed.

The Syrian general towered over Masudi, scornfully glaring at the Iranian prisoner.

The bulky, horse-faced guy in cheap East European threads—who Bolan had guessed to be the Syrians' GRU control—stood with his back to the door, observing what the Syrian had done to make Masudi scream. The GRU man idly worked crud from under his fingernails with a penknife and flipped the dirt onto the Syrian general's carpet.

The words they spoke sounded a bit clearer to Bolan this close to the window. They spoke English. Not unusual with so many nationalities warring throughout the region. Most of the participants in Lebanon's war spoke French or English, common languages often used for communication.

No sign of Strakhov.

"You have nine more fingers, General Masudi," the GRU man at the door growled without looking up from his nails. "Then I will have General Abdel begin on... more sensitive areas."

Abdel did not budge from crowding Masudi.

"It would be my pleasure, Major Kleb. It has always been my opinion that Iranians are the issue of diseased camels mating with lepers." Abdel appraised Masudi like a butcher sizing up a slab of meat. "I would take my time with this one. He would scream so much...."

The Iranian gulped and Bolan could see the terrified man's Adam's apple bobbing in his throat.

"But, Major," Masudi pleaded to the Russian around Abdel's bulk, "are we not allies? I beg of you—"

"Beg all you want," snarled the Syrian. "The Iranian Revolutionary Guards fight beside the Druse, yes, but you have never been asked into this by either our government or—" and Abdel shot a quick glance to the GRU advisor "—those of our friends. And so you will die. You will pay for your unwarranted intervention."

"We fight for the glory of Islam!" protested

Masudi. "And who has asked Syria or the Soviet Union into this?"

"Impudent swine," Abdel snarled, backhanding Masudi hard enough to send the smaller man and the chair sprawling to the floor.

Abdel pulled a booted foot back for a kick at Masudi.

The Russian officer continued to work on his nails, but spoke.

"General Abdel, one moment, please." Kleb folded and pocketed the penknife and gazed coolly at Masudi. The Iranian wiped blood from his face. "The Disciples of Allah," Kleb said in a monotone. "Tell me what you know of them, General, and perhaps we will let you live."

"The Disciples? Th-there is no such group," Masudi gasped, working to get his breath back. "It is a temporary name...nothing more than a loose band. Shiites and Druse. I have only heard of them. They carry out raids, yes, suicide fighters...but the Disciples of Allah is but a name to give the impression of greater numbers, you understand?"

Abdel eyed the Russian.

Kleb nodded.

The Syrian knelt across Masudi's chest and grabbed the Iranian's right hand.

Bolan, from his perch outside the window on the ledge, clearly heard something snap above Masudi's bleat as the Syrian broke another finger.

"He screams like a woman, this one," Abdel snickered, standing again. "He will scream the truth."

"We know when you lie, you see, General Masudi,"

Kleb said, chuckling. "We know of the plot to assassinate the Lebanese president. We know of the Disciples' part in this. We know of your role—that of sponsor and protector to these madmen. Now I want you to tell me the rest of it. All of it."

Masudi forced himself to his knees. He looked utterly defeated, but Bolan discerned a fierce determination on the man's features.

"But I . . . I do not understand. The government befriends Israel and the devil nation, America . . . surely we fight on the same side, Muslim brothers . . . the Disciples strike for us!"

"You will be tortured until you tell us what we wish to know," Kleb continued in his monotone. "General Abdel, commence, and do not stop until he talks."

"With pleasure, Major."

The Syrian bent to his task.

The bloodied Masudi got a new glint in his pain-clouded eyes and somehow, despite the oddly protruding broken digits of his right hand, he no longer looked defeated at all.

"You shall never stop us!" he screamed and rocketed to his feet before Abdel could reach him. "There are others. We are Shiites! We die for Islam! Allah be praised!"

Abdel rushed forward, grabbing for Masudi.

The Iranian twisted away from the outstretched hands while his uninjured hand darted down inside his left boot.

The GRU man at the door lost all his cool then and dived for concealed hardware. But it all happened too fast.

The Syrian general twisted around almost as fast as Masudi and clamped both hamlike hands around the Iranian's neck. Abdel grunted a curse in Arabic and yanked the smaller man around.

The Iranian allowed himself to be swung. He used the momentum to plunge a stiletto to the hilt under Abdel's breastbone, into the heart.

Abdel froze, a surprised look on his face. Then his hands dropped and a fountain of blood burbled from his mouth. The Syrian commander fell, dead.

The Iranian whirled again and with a shriek charged the Russian major, who had his pistol only half way out of its shoulder holster.

Kleb's eyes widened with panic.

The Shiite attacked him with the flashing blade.

From his perch position on the ledge outside the window Bolan witnessed and reacted instantly to the eruption of violence.

But the most vital question remained unanswered.

Where the hell was Strakhov?

10

Greb Strakhov grasped the door handle, about to step into General Abdel's office, when shouts and scuffling noises from within made him halt. He had been to the communications room downstairs, coding his report to the Soviet Embassy in Beirut for immediate transmission to Moscow.

His recent tenure behind a desk had not dulled reflexes earned during twenty years of KGB fieldwork.

The spy master tugged out his pistol.

Something heavy thumped into the corridor wall alongside the door inside that office.

Strakhov opened that door and burst in fast, cautious, just in time.

He took it in at a glance: Abdel dead on the floor across the office like a gutted fish. The impact Strakhov heard on the wall had been General Masudi throwing himself at Kleb. They piled into the wall before tumbling to the carpeted floor, locked in combat. The Iranian was on top, one fist in an iron grip on the Russian officer's gun wrist, preventing Kleb from completing his draw. Masudi was trying to force a bloodied stiletto down into Kleb's heart. The GRU man only barely fended him off with a straight-armed grip around Masudi's wrist.

HE'S EXPLOSIVE. HE'S MACK BOLAN... AGAINST ALL ODDS

He learned his deadly skills in Vietnam...then put them to good use by destroying the Mafia in a blazing one-man war. Now **Mack Bolan** ventures further into the cold to take on his deadliest challenge yet—the KGB's worldwide terror machine.

Follow the lone warrior on his exciting new missions...and get ready for more nonstop action from his high-powered combat teams: **Able Team**—Bolan's famous Death Squad—battling urban savagery too brutal and volatile for regular law enforcement. And **Phoenix Force**—five extraordinary warriors handpicked by Bolan to fight the dirtiest of antiterrorist wars, blazing into even greater danger.

Fight alongside these three courageous forces for freedom in all-new action-packed novels! Travel to the gloomy depths of the cold Atlantic, the scorching sands of the Sahara, and the desolate Russian plains. You'll feel the pressure and excitement building page after page, with nonstop action that keeps you enthralled until the explosive conclusion!

Now you can have all the new Gold Eagle novels delivered right to your home!

You won't want to miss a single one of these exciting new action-adventures. And you don't have to! Just fill out and mail the card at right, and we'll enter your name in the Gold Eagle home subscription plan. You'll then receive six brand-new action-packed Gold Eagle books every other month, delivered right to your home! You'll get two Mack Bolan novels, one Able Team and one Phoenix Force, plus one book each from two thrilling, new Gold Eagle libraries, **SOBs** and **Track**. In **SOBs** you'll meet the legendary team of mercenary warriors who fight for justice and win. **Track** features a military and weapons genius on a mission to stop a maniac whose dream is everybody's worst nightmare. Only Track stands between us and nuclear hell!

FREE! The New War Book and Mack Bolan bumper sticker.

As soon as we receive your card we'll rush you the long-awaited New War Book and Mack Bolan bumper sticker—both ABSOLUTELY FREE! Then under separate cover, you'll receive your six Gold Eagle novels.

The New War Book is *packed* with exciting information for Bolan fans: a revealing look at the hero's life...two new short stories...book character biographies...even a combat catalog describing weapons used in the novels! The New War Book is a special collector's item you'll want to read again and again. And it's yours FREE when you mail your card!

Of course, you're under no obligation to buy anything. Your first six books come on a 10-day free trial—if you're not thrilled with them, just return them and owe nothing. The New War Book and bumper sticker are yours to keep, FREE!

Don't miss a single one of these thrilling novels...mail the card now, while you're thinking about it.

GET THE NEW WAR BOOK AND
BUMPER STICKER
FREE! See exciting
details inside.

"LIVE LARGE" Mack Bolan

The closed window across the office showed the first glow of dawn. No one came in that way to help Masudi, thought Strakhov as he rushed to Kleb's aid. Masudi had hidden the dagger before they brought him into the room. The Syrians had not searched him properly. Strakhov detested all Arabs.

He hurried over and brought the butt of his pistol down hard behind Masudi's right ear, but not hard enough to kill.

The blade dropped from the Iranian's hand. Masudi collapsed sideways.

Kleb pushed him away and scrambled to his feet, yanking his gun out the rest of the way, too fast for Strakhov to stop him.

"Kleb! No!" Strakhov shouted.

The blast from Kleb's Walther PPK drowned out the command and brought death to Ib Masudi, the projectiles devouring the Iranian general's throat and part of his face.

Strakhov reached Kleb and angrily smashed the pistol from Kleb's fingers with his own Walther.

"You fool!" Strakhov snarled, lapsing into Russian.

"He...he was about to kill me," gasped Kleb.

"You were in no danger—you panicked. Now we will learn nothing from Masudi. I had the communications room monitor your interrogation in my absence. He said there are other plotters. He could have told us so much."

"I'm sorry, comrade Major General." The GRU man backed down. "I—I overreacted. But, if I may ask, after tomorrow— and dawn is only a few minutes from now— will the president's fate be of any concern to us?''

"I would not expect your peasant mind to grasp the finer points of my mission, Major," Strakhov snapped. "Do you think, if things go as we plan, that the Disciples of Allah and the other groups like them will simply disband and disappear? Or the Iranians? We must gain control of these factions now, while the power base is fluid. The ruling government in Beirut must not be slaughtered. We can only accomplish our goals away from world attention."

"I—I understand, comrade Major General."

Strakhov holstered his pistol.

"Retrieve your weapon then. What has been done cannot be undone."

Kleb obeyed meekly.

"Thank you, comrade."

"I will be taking over General Abdel's office for my stay in this pit," Strakhov growled, striding briskly with barely a glance at the dead Syrian to a chair behind the desk. "He won't be needing it." He glared daggers at Kleb. "Contact ranking officers of the Druse, Syrian, PLO and Iranian forces in the area. Schedule an emergency briefing. Here, at noon today."

"That, uh, may be difficult, comrade Major General, considering—"

"Tell them they *will* be here," Strakhov barked. "They will understand. And they will understand what I tell them at the briefing. Or they shall be replaced."

"I shall see to it immediately."

"Also see to this," Strakhov instructed. He handed

Kleb a scrap of paper. "We have traced the license number of a car seen leaving the Iranian compound at Biskinta two hours prior to our attack this morning. It was an unmarked vehicle of the Lebanese government."

Kleb registered a puzzled frown.

"The government?"

"Apparently there are things happening in Beirut at this moment that we do not know. A situation I find untenable."

"I shall...pursue the matter vigorously," Kleb promised.

"See that you do, Major, and perhaps I shall have reason to be more generous in my report concerning you to Moscow than I have thus far had reason to be. And see that these, er, things—" Strakhov indicated with disdain the two corpses "—are removed. The sight of them alive turned my stomach. Now they're worse. Tie the Iranian's neck with rope to the back of a vehicle and have him dragged through the countryside. He will be a lesson. I suppose we must be more subdued with General Abdel. Return the body to his family."

"As you wish, comrade Major General."

Kleb saluted smartly and fled the room.

Leaving Strakhov alone with the dead.

And the new dawn beginning to stretch beyond the mountains to the east.

THE EXECUTIONER had been about to storm through that window into Abdel's office in an attempt to save Masudi's life. At least until the Iranian spilled what he knew about a plot to assassinate the Lebanese president.

Then Bolan would deal with Strakhov.

He checked his move, though, when the door of the office flew inward and Strakhov barged in.

The penetrator on the ledge paused. He could continue to maintain this low profile and eavesdrop. Strakhov would want Masudi alive for the same reasons as Bolan.

When Kleb killed Masudi, too fast for anyone to stop him, Bolan winced at the Russian major's miscalculation, but like Strakhov the Executioner understood that what had happened could not be undone.

He remained listening on that ledge, the Beretta poised.

The first light of dawn began to half illuminate the Syrian base. Birds chirped. The barracks beyond Bolan's line of vision started waking up.

Bolan had better than working knowledge of Russian both written and spoken, and continued to work to master it during any available moment. He knew enough, however, to decipher the main ideas of most conversations he heard in the language and that included enough of the exchange between the two Russians in the late General Abdel's office.

Bolan now knew he could not kill the man he had come all this way to find and terminate.

The Executioner had traveled halfway around the world to this hellground and had his target under the gun, only to discover at that precise moment that The Executioner and the top savage of them all were allies with the same objective: to halt the assassination of the president of this undersized powder keg on the Mediterranean.

Bolan appreciated that ultimate stabilization of the region could only result in diplomacy. Events were overtaking themselves. There was nothing for the powder keg to do now but blow sky high. Then the diplomats could come in.

America would have to exert her influence in other ways, but it could be done. That's what diplomats did. Bolan's mission to terminate Strakhov had become Bolan's bid at making this part of the world safe for diplomacy.

As the exchange in the office ended, with Strakhov seated at that desk while Kleb scurried off, Bolan pulled back from the window and prepared to withdraw, formulating strategy on the move. He pulled back to the open window along the ledge.

He knew where he would be at noon today, if he lived that long.

Right here.

Strakhov had called an emergency summit of *all* the terrorist factions. The Syrian base at Zahle would be crawling with more of these vermin than Bolan could ever hope or expect to find in one place at one time.

High noon in Zahle?

Yeah, Bolan would be there.

Bet on it.

In the meantime, he intended to devote his energies to what had suddenly made him an ally of the cannibal chief he had come here to kill.

He had those blueprints snatched from Biskinta and the lead from Strakhov of an unmarked government car tonight where it had no business being—at an Iranian camp in the Shouf, well behind Syrian and Druse lines.

Strakhov's presence in Lebanon indicated how important the Kremlin considered his mission to consolidate these terrorist factions. It would be in the Soviets' interest to eradicate the more volatile, unpredictable element like the Disciples of Allah, giving Syria carte blanche to escalate hostilities against Israel, paving the way for an expansion of control into the Persian Gulf. Some thirty thousand Israeli troops had already been massed along the Israel-Lebanon border.

In those terms Bolan recognized the magnitude of his own mission in blocking this power play, yet he also appreciated that even when he hit Strakhov—and, damn right, Bolan intended to live that long and damn large while he was at it—The Executioner would only be hacking off one more tentacle of a hydra he had given up everything else to fight.

He would find a way.

He would find Zoraya and little Selim, too.

But first he had to get the hell out of Zahle.

At least General Masudi had not bothered to tell Strakhov of the blacksuited nightfighter who interrupted that briefing of the Disciples of Allah before they could leave Biskinta. Bolan now knew their mission could only have been part of the Shiite assassination plot to kill the president. Masudi probably mistook the commando in blackface as one of the Syrians' strike force.

Bolan almost made the open window along that second-story ledge of the headquarters building. He intended to retrace his route at least part of the way off the base.

The sun would not show itself for a while although the morning was getting lighter by the second. There were still shadows and gloom and the eye had to strain to discern things.

A three-man sentry patrol of Syrian soldiers rounded the near side of the building when the penetrator had only three or four seconds to go to reach that open window and disappear out of sight. The soldiers were marching abreast, AK-47s slung over their shoulders. The man in the middle gazed up almost idly at the lighted window of General Abdel's office and the other two looked with him. Just one of those things.

Two minutes earlier it would have been dark enough for the nightstriker to go undetected from down there, but Bolan had stayed too long in the heart of the enemy camp.

The sentries saw him.

11

Bolan jumped off the ledge feet first into the trio of soldiers before any of them could utter a sound or swing their rifles up at the blacksuited blur that descended upon them.

He could have attempted to pick them off from his perch with the Beretta—he had that much of an advantage before the soldiers saw him. But he knew Strakhov, in that office, would hear the silenced chugging of the Beretta, and Bolan much preferred to keep this as quiet as possible until the appropriate moment.

Two of the soldiers blocked Bolan's fall when the heel of each boot caught a man in the forehead with enough force to impact skullbone deep into brain matter, rendering those two instantly lifeless.

The momentum of the fall carried Bolan into a somersault, which he came out of just as the third soldier managed, while opening his mouth to shout an alarm, to begin tracking his AK on Bolan.

Bolan moved lightning fast, his left foot coming up in a high martial-arts kick that deflected the soldier's assault rifle, knocking it from the man's hands.

Bolan regained his balance and jabbed his right hand straight and hard in another thrust to crush the soldier's Adam's apple, cutting off the warning before it began. Then The Executioner brought his left hand down in a hard chop, breaking the man's neck, and the sentry collapsed on top of the other two, not quite as bloody but just as dead.

Bolan took off, running across the tarmac toward the Russian tanks and munitions he had spotted coming in. He knew those tanks would be rolling in another hour or two, carrying more death in the world so the cannibals could grab a few more inches on the world map.

A much better use for those war machines would be as a diversion, Bolan decided. He extracted a wad of wrapped plastique as he moved toward them through the growing light of approaching dawn.

The motor pool sat next to that Soviet weaponry, he recalled, and most of the base security had been deployed along the perimeter....

A two-man patrol emerged from between the rows of parked tanks when Bolan had only fifty paces to go. They saw him in the dawn's early light. They were holding their AKs at port arms. The two rifles leveled as one on the figure in blacksuit, the Syrian soldiers diving sideways.

Bolan assumed a combat shooting stance, steadied his aim with his left hand and the Beretta spit its muted death yip in the quiet air but far enough away from the barracks for the silenced chugs not to be heard.

The two soldiers twirled into a macabre ballet of death, rifles flipping away as the two bodies sank against the nearest Soviet T-55 and collapsed.

Their corpses were still trembling with the shock of death as the Executioner buzzed past, stooping without slowing after he holstered the Beretta to grab up one of the AKs and one soldier's hip-clipped ammo pack.

Time for the heavy stuff.

It took less than thirty seconds to unwrap the plastique and place the puttylike explosive between the crawler tracks of one of the tanks.

He found the ammunition dump in the center of the row of tanks. The ammo stash had a two-man guard. These Syrians were leaning against a T-55, chatting idly with no idea of their approaching death.

Bolan rifle-butted the soldier nearest him across the back of the head and heard skullbone crack.

The second man started to react to the strange sounds from his buddy when Death jerked the AK-47 sideways in one continuous motion from the first kill, smashing the rifle butt into the second soldier's head, killing him, too.

Bolan spent eleven seconds planting the remainder of his plastique around the stash of rockets. He set the timer in this death putty for the appropriate seconds to coincide with what he left on the tank.

Thirty seconds to blast-off.

The sun splashed its first red traces over the hills to the east.

Bolan dashed from the tarmac toward the collection of jeeps and trucks around the two-bay garage of the base motor pool.

Four sleepy-eyed regulars were loitering around a coffeepot, girding themselves for another day of war. When they saw Bolan on his dash toward a line of jeeplike vehicles, the soldiers all swung simultaneously, coming wide awake. They dropped their coffee mugs and reached for weapons as the air clouded with spraying coffee and blood. The AK-47 yammered in Bolan's grip as he rode the heavy recoil of the assault rifle.

Bodies tumbled in the garage like a little St. Valentine's Day massacre. The big fighter in blacksuit leaped into the nearest jeep and found the keys in the ignition as he expected.

He paused only to slam a fresh magazine into the AK. Then he gunned the vehicle to life and stormed the hell out of there along a roadway that bisected the compound and led to the gate.

The hammering of his AK had alerted the camp.

Soldiers poured out from every building on the compound, freshly awakened and in various stages of dress, but every one of them carrying a weapon. Most were well behind the speeding jeep.

Bolan roared full speed toward the main gate. He heard some firing at him from behind, but none of the whizzing projectiles came near man or rocketing vehicle.

The gate sentries and the men in the sandbag- encircled machine-gun nests adjacent to the entrance guardhouse responded to something wrong, finding positions behind their weapons.

But they held their fire as the Syrian jeep bore down on them. Bolan guessed they must have figured it was one of their officers coming with orders for them. Bolan saw the officer of the guard frantically jabbering on a field phone inside a window of the guardhouse.

The Executioner would have preferred taking another way out, but because there were machine-gun emplacements along the perimeter he would still have to make it through multilayered rows of concertina wire. He did not have that kind of time before the troops behind him in the compound amassed with their own vehicles and gave chase.

Then there came a deafening blast from the direction of the Russian tanks and munitions. The explosion shook the earth beneath everyone with a deep-throated roar and the tarmac area exploded into brilliant, blinding flame, blue-black smoke billowing straight up to blot out the rising sun.

It was the diversion Bolan needed.

Knowing the earth-shuddering blast would hit, Bolan did not look toward the area the way everyone else did, including the soldiers stationed at the gate.

It took only the blink of an eye for every man there to whip his attention and weapons back toward the approaching Syrian vehicle. But by that time Bolan had steered the jeep into a sideways skid and heaved three of the grenades he carried.

The first one sailed through the window of the guardhouse where the officer had forgotten his field phone, drawing a bead on Bolan with a pistol. The second landed unerringly into the nearest machine-gun nest, and the last grenade dropped at the base of the mesh-wire gates.

The machine-gun nest of soldiers seemed almost to implode under the force of a blast intensified in the confines of the sandbags.

The officer of the guard and his flimsy guardhouse

disintegrated, and Bolan sought cover behind his vehicle as the earth rumbled again and pieces of building and bodies and the main gate rained down upon him.

No gunfire issued from drifting clouds that were all that remained of the gate, the machine-gun nest and everything else that had barred his withdrawal.

He launched himself behind the wheel of the jeep and flung a human arm, severed at the shoulder, the fingers still fluttering spasmodically, from where it had landed in the passenger seat. Then he steered the vehicle pell-mell through those drifting clouds.

The jeep bumped over the gaping pothole left by the explosion that had demolished the gate.

He risked a glance back over his shoulder as he steered up the incline leading from the valley of Zahle and the Syrian base.

From the high ground as the jeep bounced along, he could see the tanks and munitions on the tarmac being eaten up, incinerated by hungry flames that some of the surviving soldiers were fighting to extinguish before the blaze spread.

Other soldiers were piling into the remaining vehicles at the motor-pool garage.

Getting ready for hot pursuit.

MAJOR GENERAL STRAKHOV charged from the headquarters building less than thirty seconds after the explosions had rocked the base.

The compound looked like a hive of insane bees. Syrian soldiers and Russian advisors were scurrying everywhere in the confusion, trying to find an enemy to fight. The light of the new day bathed an inferno ten times as bright when secondary explosions blew up the tarmac and stung Strakhov's eardrums.

He hurried to the motor-pool garage where he saw Major Kleb and two of the GRU man's Russian subordinates trying to establish some order, dead bodies and destruction everywhere.

Strakhov raised his voice above the melee.

"Major! What is going on here?"

Kleb's face shone in the flames around him, covered with sweat and soot, his eyes wild.

"An attack, comrade Major General!"

"I can see that, idiot! How many of them were there? Were any apprehended?"

Kleb nodded to the Syrian officers ordering their men into troop trucks.

"I have instructed them to give chase, as you can see. Those who saw the attack say it was the work of one man."

"One man?" Strakhov echoed, gazing incredulously at the damage and bodies and fury of flames from the tarmac and the gate. "Preposterous!"

"Uh, er, yes, my sentiments exactly, comrade Major General. Nonetheless, as you can see, he, or, uh, they. . . shall not get far."

Four troop carriers gunned their engines in final preparation for frantic pursuit.

Strakhov grabbed the lapel of Kleb's tunic and shook him with barely contained rage.

"Fool! Send one truck, imbecile. This could be a trick. A trap to lure us away. Triple the security around the perimeter. Have all officers report to me in the headquarters building immediately."

Kleb saluted. "As you wish, comrade Major General."

Strakhov turned and stormed back into the HQ building, wondering how the attackers had managed to breach the tight security measures and wreak such havoc.

He did not for a moment believe one man could possibly be responsible for all this.

As HE DROVE, Bolan found he had no difficulty remembering this route. He had paid close attention to the road into the base less than an hour ago, as the driver of the troop truck. He had memorized the prime spots for an ambush along the way. Now that paid off. In another hour or less these hilly back roads would be swarming with soldiers, but now he had this road to himself as he coaxed more speed from his vehicle, pedal to metal.

When he did approach Beirut and the Phalangist positions, he would need to ditch the jeep, of course, but in his withdrawal from the Shouf, these wheels could serve him well. And if he encountered Druse or Syrian checkpoints and the Syrian army markings did not do the trick, well, he had the Beretta and Big Thunder and the AK-47.

He negotiated a down-curving bend and found a spot he remembered.

He tromped on the brakes and his vehicle shuddered to a grinding stop, halting sideways across the road.

Bolan scrambled from behind the steering wheel and hustled up a steep incline beyond the culvert on one side of the road to a rim of wild shrubbery.

He would have less than a minute before his pursuers rattled around that bend after him. Bolan hoped like hell they had not sent more than a truck or two, which could be manageable.

With General Abdel dead Strakhov would assume temporary command back there, until the Syrian chain of command realigned itself after the Executioner's hellfire.

The Russians called themselves "advisors," sure, but everyone knew who really called the shots and that would go double for a VIP from the head shed.

A hothead Syrian might send every trooper on the base in pursuit of Bolan, but coolheaded Strakhov would know better. He did not yet know of Bolan's presence in the area and would read this hit-and-git strike as possibly the work of government commandos testing the reflexes of the enemy preparatory to a follow-up strike.

Strakhov would most likely send a squadron after the stolen vehicle, but with the main force remaining at Zahle.

Pebbles and small rocks skittered down the incline behind Bolan's hurried climb, when a troop carrier came roaring down the grade and around the bend. The driver was too busy negotiating the turn and braking to keep his truck on the road and not hit the jeep to notice the telltale traces of an ambush setup.

Bolan had the AK-47 ready from cover shrubbery on the high ground overlooking the road. He had parked his vehicle far enough from the curve in the road to allow the driver to halt his truck without crashing into the jeep, but close enough to fully occupy the driver's attention.

The troop truck fishtailed to a stop.

There were angry shouts from the men in the rear.

Then those shouts and everything else got buried beneath the bucking reports of Bolan's rifle as he riddled the cab of the truck, pulverizing windshield and the heads of the driver and another man in a shower of glass and gore.

The Executioner came loping down the incline as two soldiers started climbing out frantically from under the tarp at the back of the truck. Bolan squeezed the AK's trigger, and twin sprouts the color of the red dawn exploded from shattered bodies that collapsed like discarded toys onto the road behind the vehicle.

Bolan approached the troop carrier and underhanded a grenade into the rear of the truck before anyone else could try to get out. Then it was too late for any of them to do anything but disintegrate. The blast catapulted the carrier onto its side, leaving the tarp, machine and occupants in shredded ruins. The explosion echoed from mountain to mountain.

Bolan hurried back to the jeep, which he had left idling, and got the hell away from there before any more trucks decided to give chase when they got no word from this one.

He had to get back to Beirut, the city of hate.

Back to where the hellfire flamed hottest.

For the mission; for Zoraya and Selim.

For Lebanon.

For the War Everlasting against cannibals like Greb Strakhov and everything that ultimate savage stood for.

A new day, right.

A new war.

The Bastard in Black would see them both through to the bloody finish.

12

Bob Collins awoke with a start and reached for the .45 automatic he always wore in a shoulder holster. He relaxed when he realized Al Randolph was the man shaking him awake. Collins sat up on the cot in their "office" and blinked the sleep from his eyes.

He and Randolph were partners and sort of friends, CIA agents who had risen through the ranks to find themselves stuck with the worst assignment of all.

"What the hell is it?"

The sleep had been fitful but welcome just the same, a respite from Hell. Collins and Randolph had not only been stuck with the undesirable job, but were right smack in the middle of it and there was no escape at all.

"Wake up." Randolph shook him some more. "We've got trouble."

Collins reoriented himself to the CIA monitoring station: the basement of a closed vegetable business owned by a Company front in the Christian sector of Beirut. Like living in a dungeon, Collins thought again. Then he shook the depression and glowered.

"Okay, Al. Trouble. Trouble in Hell. Give it a name."

"Bolan," Randolph replied, and that woke Collins

up all the way. Randolph moved to lean his bulk against the battered table in the corner where they kept the scrambler phone to the embassy. He lit a cigarette. "Just got it. Thought you'd want to know."

Collins turned on the hot plate to heat water for instant coffee. The cellar room felt as claustrophobic as ever.

"And I suppose our orders are to keep this sector wired for public enemy number one."

"You got it. Make that world enemy."

"I know the standing orders on the guy," Collins grouched. "Shoot on sight. I wonder what the hell Mack Bolan is doing in Beirut, now that he's put himself against the KGB. They're all over this rathole, sure, but nothing that hasn't been going on for a long, long time. Maybe our buddies in Mossad know."

Randolph grunted and lit another butt.

"Buddies, uh-huh. Depending on which way the wind is blowing out of Washington and Tel Aviv this hour. And I don't think we're going to be such buddies with Mossad after you hear the rest of what I just got."

Collins spooned coffee into a cup, added hot water and stirred.

"So tell me, Al. We've got to hit the streets in the middle of everything that's going to bust loose today, keep our cover intact and monitor the fighting and not get killed. Now we've got Mack Bolan and orders to terminate a guy the Vietcong, the Mafia and all the terrorists in the world couldn't kill. A guy who was on our side until a few months ago and maybe he still is. And you say you've got something else." Collins looked at his partner. "Maybe we ought to pack a suitcase and slip out and go home, Al. You ever thought of that?

"What the hell brought us into this, anyway? A few months ago this guy Bolan would've come to us for help. Now we're supposed to kill him. And all the rest of it. I don't want to die in Beirut. Do you want to die in Beirut? We've been conned, Al. Let's go home."

The cynicism disappeared from Randolph's face, and all of a sudden he looked honest and as tired as Collins felt.

"Dammit, stop it, Bob. Get it together. You know it's not as easy as that and it does mean something. Even if you did get out that way you'd get what Bolan got."

Collins sipped his coffee.

"You're right. Sorry about the whining, Al. It won't happen again. But you want to know something... what Bolan got ain't so bad. He's got himself, buddy. They took him but he got himself back and his name and his soul with it."

Randolph dragged on his cigarette.

"I know what you mean. We're on the same side as he is in a way, but orders are orders. The Company can't allow anyone running around tackling wild, unsanctioned actions in sensitive areas like this the way Bolan does."

"He gets results, Al. And I don't think we have to worry about too many people trying or even coming close to what Bolan has done. The Executioner is one in ten million. No, make it one of a kind. That's Bolan."

"So our orders suck," Randolph grunted and the cynical tone returned. "So call up the embassy on the scrambler and tell 'em the orders suck. And see what they give you back. These orders come from the top, pally. And the orders say: terminate Bolan."

"I said I know the orders. And you said you had something else about Mossad. So we don't share our intel with them. So how worse can it get?"

"Does the name Katzenelenbogen ring a bell?"

"Uh-huh. He's the honcho of the Stony Man Farm operation Bolan used to head before Bolan went lone wolf. I never heard anything bad about the Israeli."

"Lend an ear. Katz got Bolan over here using some old ties with Mossad, slipped Bolan in through Israel, and no one who helped knew the guy is on the hit list of every spy agency in existence."

"Must be something real big cooking to get Bolan in," Collins thought aloud. "That incredible dude has taken on the whole KGB. That's full-time work even for him."

"Crazy," Randolph grumbled.

"Yeah." Collins tried on the cynicism. "Crazy when he took on the whole frigging Mafia. He tore that organization of scumbags to shreds and they still haven't recovered. Crazy when he let the government talk him into taking on the worldwide terrorist network. Well, maybe he did give the government too much of his soul for a while there, but take a look at what a shambles he made of international terrorism. Was Don Quixote crazy? People are still talking about that one a couple of hundred years later for inspiration."

Randolph started to light a third cigarette but threw it away in disgust.

"Damn things. I'll die of cancer before the guns get me." He looked at Collins. "The only way it figures is that Bolan hasn't tackled our local KGB opposite numbers up to now because the situation has been too damn fluid for anyone to get a handle on it, including Bolan."

"And now he's got the handle and we don't know what the hell it is," Collins muttered. "You're saying whatever has brought Bolan here came from Mossad, through Katzenelenbogen?"

"I'm saying what Control told me."

"And our orders?"

"We have a fix on Katzenelenbogen. He's with an Israeli military unit across the border. We pick him up. We interrogate him. Mossad will cooperate."

Collins finished his coffee and set the empty cup down with a clunk.

"Mossad might cooperate. Katzenelenbogen won't. Neither will Bolan. Not by a damn sight."

"Right. That's what I told Control, but those bastards never listen to advice from the street."

From somewhere above came the yammer of automatic weapons. Randolph thought it sounded strangely removed from their subterranean station, yet uncomfortably near. Too near.

Shouts and answering gunfire rang through the streets.

As on virtually all of the stores in the city, the sliding metal garage-doorlike front had been pulled down on the vegetable store. It had not been open for weeks, since the latest outbreak of serious fighting.

Collins glanced at his wristwatch, then in the direction of the warfare, as if he could see through the clay walls of the cellar.

"Hell, it's only 5:00 A.M. They're starting early today."

"We can get out now," Randolph suggested. He grabbed Collins's jacket from a peg and tossed it to him. "We'll be back by early afternoon."

"Is that Control's idea or yours?"

"Coming back? That's the mission, isn't it? We've still got the mission. And there's Bolan."

Collins flicked off the cellar light. They started up the stairs toward the back entrance of the building.

"I've got a feeling," Collins told his partner, "there'll always be a Bolan. That bastard's too damn mean to die."

"Sir, the call you've been waiting for is on the field phone."

Yakov Katzenelenbogen nodded and grabbed the phone's receiver.

Katz was certain the caller would be Mack Bolan. It would be the first time they made contact since the Phoenix Force leader and the Executioner had parted ways along the Israel-Lebanon border hours earlier. At that time, Bolan had been on his way to meet Yakov's nephew, Chaim.

This call would be from Bolan's miniature transceiver, boosted and scrambled by several Israeli stations until relayed through the wires to this communications tent on the Israeli army base at Acre.

Katz had expected to hear from Bolan well before

this and had tried to ignore the worry that plagued him. The thirty thousand Israeli troops had been massed along the border with good reason. Things were going to hell in a hand basket in Lebanon.

The first light of day warmed comfortably, but Katz felt cold inside.

"Go," he growled curtly into the field phone receiver.

"Mack here."

Katz casually turned away from the others in the communications tent and pitched his voice low.

"What have you got, Striker?"

"Bad news, Yakov. Chaim is dead."

The Israeli's throat constricted.

"How? Strakhov?"

"No. Chaim got hit in a cross fire between Druse and Phalangists."

"The woman, Zoraya?"

Katz kept his voice hard. The senior member of Phoenix Force had been losing members of his family to violence since World War II, leaving him to carry the pain. He had almost gotten used to it. Almost.

"I had Zoraya and I lost her," Bolan replied.

"Then you've got her again. She contacted Chaim's control officer in Beirut not ten minutes ago. He got the message to me and I got back to her. She...said nothing about Chaim."

"She probably didn't know how to. I know how she felt. What did she say?"

"That you must contact her." Katz gave Bolan the address in Beirut that Zoraya had given him. "She wouldn't stay on. Chaim's control can't get to her. You must know how the situation is there. He's unable to move anywhere.''

"I'll get to her," Bolan promised.

"And your target?"

"Still at large. I had him under the gun, but I gave him a white flag without him knowing it. The enemy is on our side of the street this once. For a few hours, anyway. There's a plot to hit the Lebanese president, but Moscow thinks it's the wrong time. They've sent our man to straighten it out.''

"Any leads?"

"The Disciples of Allah."

"The ones who—"

"Right. Only the bunch I found tonight won't be massacring any more Marines or anyone else.''

Katz started to ask what Bolan intended to do next when he noticed three men strutting toward him with grim determination: the commander of this Israeli detachment and two men in American civilian apparel whom Katz read as CIA.

He lowered his voice even more and spoke rapidly into the mouthpiece.

"Trouble, Mack. I'm about to be arrested and interrogated, if I read this right. Uh, if I allow it, that is. How do I play it?"

Katz had only seconds before the three men reached him. They would not buy his beret-topped professorial air but would know exactly how dangerous he was. All three of them carried pistols. What they did not, could not, know was that Katz already had them under the gun.

The one-armed ex-Mossad boss wore a prosthetic device attached to the stump of his right arm. This "hand," a state-of-the-art contraption of steel, insulated wires and cables with four fingers and a thumb, was not as practical or versatile as the three-pronged hook Katz favored.

But the device featured an "index finger" that was in fact the barrel of a built-in, single-shot pistol that fired a .22 Magnum cartridge. The bullet was detonated by a nine-volt battery that could be activated by manipulation of the muscles in the stump of Katz's arm. There was a safety catch at the palm of the artificial hand to prevent firing the gun by accident.

Katz computed the odds of grabbing his holstered pistol while two of these men recovered if he fired the "index finger" at one of them, but of course that was only reflex thinking. He could not fire on these men and he knew it.

Bolan's voice crackled over the field phone.

"Cooperate with them like a stone wall. I need time, Yakov. Can you do it and not jeopardize your Stony Man position?"

The Israeli chuckled grimly.

"You do your job, Striker, I'll do mine."

He hung up the phone as the three men reached him.

"Yes, gentlemen?"

"Colonel Katzenelenbogen," began the Israeli officer, "these men are American CIA. Mr. Collins and Mr. Randolph. Mossad has ordered me to cooperate with them fully."

"And those guns you're carrying say I cooperate

with you fully, is that it?'' Katz retorted. ''Very well. Let's hear what you have to say.''

Katz hoped these three and those who would certainly continue to interrogate him after these guys were done would not see through his stone wall.

Mack Bolan had just lost his one contact out of Lebanon.

13

Bolan abandoned the Syrian jeep well before he reached the city. Twice on foot he dodged military patrols—one Syrian, the other Druse—and it was only because of the ever shifting lines that he was able to move at all.

At a farmhouse he offered a Muslim family more Lebanese pounds than they probably saw in a year for the rusty Saab that had only one fender and no lights. They were glad to take the money and Bolan took the car, continuing on into Beirut.

The address Zoraya had given Katz was in Hay al-Salloum, an area generally under the control of the Shiite militia group called Amal.

Centuries of punishing white sun and winds had razored across the neighborhood like the breath of Hades. The area, which had also fallen victim to war, was not very different from the section where Zoraya lived near the Avenue des Français, except that Hay al-Salloum appeared to be a more commercial district. But it was every bit as closed up and deserted as that corner of the hellground where Bolan had last met Zoraya.

Today's shelling of the city had begun when Bolan got within two blocks of the place his map of Beirut indicated he would find Zoraya and perhaps the child, Selim.

Thoughts of the woman and boy left Bolan's mind when the bombardment from Druse artillery in the mountains resumed, aimed at the Christian sectors of the city and government positions. Yet Bolan knew war well enough to realize the shelling would be taken as a signal by all troops and gunmen in the city that the war was on for another day. The brief respite of the morning was over. The killing could resume.

Bolan parked his car and continued warily on foot, his combat blacksuit, Beretta and Big Thunder again making him appear no more out of place than he had during the hours of darkness.

The streets and avenues streamed with pedestrians, civilians, toting luggage and children, hurrying to be gone.

Bolan passed them going in the opposite direction when he heard moans and tortured pleas for help from an alley.

He paused and glanced in to see two Shiite militiamen tormenting one of their own, a veiled Muslim woman.

One of the soldiers laughed and cruelly squeezed and twisted the hapless woman's breasts through her clothes. The other Shiite forgot his grenade launcher for a moment and fumbled to unbutton the fly on his uniform with one hand. With the other he reached to pull off the woman's veil.

Bolan barely stopped. Big Thunder roared twice and two would-be rapists were deposited headless amid the bombed-out rubble. He continued on. The woman hurried away.

The address Katz had passed on to him as the

rendezvous point with Zoraya turned out to be an auto-repair garage, the metal doors closed.

Bolan tried the handle of a door set into the business front alongside the garage opening, and this portal opened inward.

The street was full of civilians, not soldiers. The gunmen of the different factions engaged one another blocks away, the sounds of the shooting muted by rows of bombed-out buildings and others like the garage that had somehow remained untouched thus far.

Bolan soundlessly closed the door behind him with his heel. Icy eyes and a cold Beretta fanned the gloom. He discerned rusted-out hulks of cars on blocks, stripped of parts over the years. There was nothing else except a table and a dim lightbulb. Then Bolan noticed a djellaba-robed Arab who stood tentatively watching the fearsome combat figure approach him.

Another small business chewed up and spit out by the ravages of war.

"Yes, effendi, may I be of service?" The Arab's eyes took in Bolan's weapons fearfully.

"You address me in English," Bolan noted. "I am the one you expect. Where is Zoraya?"

Relief shone in the old man's eyes, then reverted to paranoia again as he glanced cautiously back in the direction of the door.

"You were not followed?"

"There are no government soldiers behind me."

"Bah! We have as much to fear from Amal and the Druse!" the old man spit.

He walked over and locked the street door, then returned and spryly stepped up onto the table. He used a pocketknife to pry open a break that looked like nothing more than the juncture between ceiling and wall from where Bolan stood. The old man tugged. A ceiling panel angled down to reveal some wooden steps leading up into an attic.

The man gestured.

"If you please, effendi. I will remain down here and keep watch. Zoraya knows the signal in the event of . . . unexpected company."

Bolan acknowledged this but did not drop his wariness of the man. He climbed onto the table and up those steps.

He emerged into the secret attic space ready to blast back at any trap waiting for him.

No trap.

Zoraya waited for him.

She had been sitting on a low bed, which, with a chair and overturned orange crate for a table, were the only pieces of furniture in the slant-roofed little place. A high window in one end of the attic wall let in sunlight marred by rising clouds of battle from a neighborhood nearby. Zoraya stood and approached Bolan with a small sound of relief and happiness.

Bolan emerged fully into the attic. The hidden entrance to the room closed up after him.

He holstered the Beretta and took Zoraya in his arms. They hugged each other like dear friends who had parted and never expected to see each other again. There was nothing sexual, but no way could Bolan the man not be aware of the physical charms of this dark-haired Arab beauty.

She did not stop hugging him for long moments.

"I. . .thought I had lost you," she whispered, "as I lost Chaim! Soldiers came after you left me with Selim at Biskinta. . .a force of Syrians, Russian advisors with them. . . . You made me promise to let nothing happen to the little one. . . . I wanted to stay, but. . .they were searching the area. They fired on us as we drove away."

"You did right," he told her. "The man downstairs. Can he be trusted?"

She nodded against his shoulder.

"He is my uncle. He loved my brothers dearly and now he hates the Druse militia for what they did. . .for the murder of Adli and Aziz. He hides and protects me here. . . . There is as much rape as killing now."

Bolan remembered the action he'd halted in the alley before arriving here.

"I'm glad you're safe. Where's Selim?"

Zoraya sat back down on the bed.

"There is the good news. The government has an agency for exactly such situations: children separated from their parents and the like. I took Selim there first thing this morning when they opened and did not leave until I had their assurance that they would ascertain the whereabouts of the little one's parents. They were displaced during the fighting."

Bolan felt a weight of responsibility lift from his shoulders. He straddled the wooden chair next to the bed and faced Zoraya.

"I'm glad to hear that. And I appreciate your getting word to me the way you did through Chaim's uncle."

"I had to tell Chaim's control officer about General

Strakhov at Zahle and the Disciples of Allah in case you did not return. And...Chaim's partner told me more about you, Mack Bolan. They call you The Executioner.''

"What else did they tell you?"

"Chaim's uncle has been detained for questioning regarding your presence here and how you got into Lebanon."

"And what are your orders from Chaim's partner?" She held eye contact with him.

"To report the moment you contact me."

"And your uncle?"

"My uncle knows nothing of any of this. Mossad cooperates with your Central Intelligence Agency. They must try to stop you. But I had heard of The Executioner before this. Your name is legend, you see, even in such a wasteland as this, Mack Bolan."

"And now?"

"I am your friend," she replied without hesitation. "I knew you would return; that you would not die in Biskinta."

"Or Zahle," he added dryly. He stood up, reached inside his blacksuit and sat next to her on the edge of the bed. He unfolded the blueprints retrieved during the battle at the Iranian base and spread the plans out on the blanket. "I need you to translate something for me, Zoraya." He directed her attention to the Arabic lettering along the bottom of the sheet of paper.

She read it, then looked up with question marks in those Mediterranean eyes.

"These...are floor plans of the presidential palace at Baabda."

Bolan refolded the blueprints.

"That clinches it, then. I've got to contact Mossad with this and I'll need your help."

"I will do anything to help stop this war, as I told you. But Mossad . . . are they not your enemies, too?"

"I've got an angle on that. Tell Chaim's partner that you've got me and I wish to talk with him. Tell him I've got information on an assassination plot, but start the conversation off by saying he's not to let on to whoever he's with. Most likely he'll be with a Company man and the moment they know it's me they'll try to trace the call. Even if Chaim's partner agrees to meet me alone, the CIA wouldn't let him. They want me real bad."

"Because of what you will do?"

"Because of what I've done and what they think I am. Can you do this for me?"

"Of course. You will wait here?"

He nodded and watched her lower the hidden stairs.

"Be careful, Zoraya."

She nodded, then left him, closing the partition behind her.

Bolan stretched out on the bed, then palmed the Beretta in his right hand.

This would be a good spot for an ambush, in which case he had read Zoraya one hundred percent wrong. It was a chance he had to take.

He rested his head on the pillow, relishing these few moments away from the fray. He appreciated the opportunity to recharge his inner batteries for what stretched ahead.

Zoraya returned minutes later and reclosed the secret opening.

The distant sounds of war could have been a thousand miles away.

"Chaim's partner will meet you in ninety minutes at a pub off the Avenue des Français." She recited an address that Bolan committed to memory. "Such establishments, you see, do a wonderful business at times such as these. Those who cannot escape the city drink while they wait to live or die. He will be there at ten-thirty." She briefly described what the Mossad agent told her he would be wearing. "He says he will recognize you."

"I bet he will. What's his name?"

"Uri Weizmann. He and Chaim were very close professionally and as friends. You can trust him, Mack, believe me."

"Thanks, Zoraya."

She paused, then said, "There is...something you can do for me in return, Mack Bolan."

He gazed up at her from the bed.

"Tell me."

"If you would just...hold me," she said quietly. "I feel...so alone. Just hold me, Mack...please... nothing more...."

Bolan read the sad, lonely look in her eyes and extended his arms.

She stretched out against him atop the covers of the bed, resting tousled midnight hair into the crook of his arm. No, there was not one thing erotic about it at all, only a need for the touch of someone humane and good to somehow balance out everything else and, yes, Bolan needed that, too. They held each other for a long time in the solitude of the attic far away from the war.

They comforted each other and reaffirmed themselves as decent human beings who could care and share gentleness.

And nothing more.

14

Somehow, they were all together again at Stony Man Farm, and his heart soared with happiness for the first time in a long, long time because April was there with him.

April Rose and Konzaki and "Bear" Kurtzman.

Andrzej Konzaki, legless since Vietnam, armorer extraordinaire of the Phoenix program, exuded physical stamina from his wheelchair as he recounted a ribald joke to Kurtzman, the Farm's computer mastermind.

Kurtzman pretended the joke wasn't funny, but that was a joke, too, between the four friends on the patio on one of those rare occasions when The Executioner allowed himself to slow down between missions for some R & R—to be human again.

Bolan and April stood away from the patio and picnic table where the four of them had just devoured the steaks Bolan had prepared. The Virginia night had a pleasant coolness. Constellations spangled in the indigo heavens away from the illumination of the patio of the "rustic farmhouse" that was in fact the command center of Bolan's antiterrorist group.

Bolan stood behind April, the love of his life who was also the coordinator, the "warden" of this secret base. His arms enfolded her, the scent of her natural fragrance titillating his nostrils, his senses.

April uttered a contented sound from deep within and Bolan knew how she felt.

Everything was perfect....

The thud of an impacting mortar shell in the near distance awoke Bolan with a start. In a flash he crouched into a shooter's stance next to the bed, fanning the silenced Beretta 93-R around the attic above the garage in Beirut.

Empty.

Zoraya had gone.

Bolan blinked the sleep from his eyes and reprimanded himself, irked that he had allowed it to happen. But he had been forced during the past hours to push himself beyond endurance of even a combattoughened pro. At least the lapse into deep sleep had occurred in the safety of this refuge.

Where was Zoraya?

And then for just one heartbeat, enough of his dream of April came back to burn through his gut like a bullet, and he brushed at a tear on his cheek. He blinked it away and the iciness of the trained executioner took over.

April and Konzaki were dead, killed in the same KGB-ordered commando raid on Stony Man Farm that had left Kurtzman a wheelchair case for the rest of his life.

Bolan moved to the secret-stair panel and glanced at his digital watch as he moved.

It was 9:55 A.M.

He had not been asleep more than ten minutes. He

still had time to make the meeting Zoraya said she had arranged with the Mossad man, Weizmann, at the pub across town—a town falling to insurgents; Bolan could feel it, sense it.

He slid open the partition and lowered himself to the garage of Zoraya's uncle.

The place was empty except for the hulks of stripped vehicles and the body of the old man.

Zoraya's uncle lay sprawled on his side across the cement floor near the door, his neck twisted at an impossible angle.

Bolan stooped to check the old Muslim's pulse to make sure.

The man's neck had been broken.

A wallet lay alongside the body.

Bolan pried a quick look inside the billfold. It had been stripped of currency. The photo identification proved it to be the dead man's.

Bolan figured it three possible ways.

The enemy—anyone from the fighting factions in this civil war to sideliners like the CIA, Mossad or even Syrian Intelligence—could have spirited Zoraya away in an effort to locate Bolan. And not even the murder of her uncle had made Zoraya reveal Bolan in the hidden attic.

The enemy took her and left the uncle's empty wallet to mislead any Beirut police investigation, which wasn't very likely in the first place.

Too silent, too quick to awaken Bolan.

Damn, *damn*.

There was of course the likelihood that it had been wandering gunmen from a Muslim or Arab Christian faction who had not thought twice about snuffing a useless old man for the few Lebanese pounds he might carry.

And the final possibility.

Zoraya could have killed the old man.

Bolan wished like hell that he could rid his mind of these ungrateful thoughts about tough, brave, humane Zoraya, but he had a realistic sense of his importance to the real enemy.

Strakhov's KGB had a special unit assigned to terminate Bolan in revenge for Bolan's killing Strakhov's only son.

Considering the elaborate steps taken to frame Bolan for the CIA a while back, it only made sense they could consider and implement a similarly complex operation. But before terminating Bolan they would torture out of him what he knew of the operations of the U.S. intelligence community from his time as "John Phoenix."

Zoraya's uncle could have discovered this and threatened to tell Bolan and, yeah, that would get the old guy killed.

Bolan did not have the time to pursue any of these possibilities. He had a Mossad agent to meet.

Unless that was part of the trap, too.

The shifting quicksand of this mission was as unpredictable as the future of Lebanon itself.

He stood up from the body and started toward the door leading out to the street.

The door burst open.

Bolan froze and dropped to a combat crouch, 93-R in hand, ready to kill.

Two veiled Muslim women, surrounded by seven scrambling children, burst into what they thought to be a temporary refuge.

Gunfire erupted outside.

The group regarded with wide eyes the dead body and the imposing sight of the warrior.

Bolan lowered the pistol, motioning them inside. Seeing the gun, the refugees obeyed, breath caught in their throats, waiting for whatever would happen next. Their faces registered surprise when Bolan trotted out.

A military vehicle with two Muslim gunmen moved leisurely down the middle of the street, punks looking to prey on refugees, such as those who had dodged into the safety of the garage.

The gunmen saw Bolan. The driver braked and reached for his rifle. His buddy bandit scrambled to a mounted machine gun on the back of their vehicle.

Bolan holstered the Beretta and shifted to the Auto-Mag. A pair of well-aimed shots wasted the duo.

He had to kill another three—Phalangists this time. He could have talked his way past, except that they opened fire on him before he had the chance. Bolan had no alternative if he wanted to live.

He arrived at the battered Saab he had bought from the family outside town. Bolan was sure no one had tampered with the decrepit vehicle.

He climbed in and started on his way.

Beirut presented a strange paradox. Although a civil war raged in its midst for control of the city itself, and the streets hosted an ever increasing number of refugees, you could turn a corner and find yourself stalled by rubble, bombed-out buildings and sniper fire. But you could also reverse your route and travel for blocks along peaceful thoroughfares just like those in any city anywhere.

Strange, yeah.

And very deadly.

From everything Bolan could see, today's action in the city equaled last night's fighting in intensity. Mortar and artillery shells fell with unsettling regularity. Dark smoke clouds blotted out the sun, intensifying the brassy heat.

There were no clearly demarcated battle lines between the fighting factions. Gunmen of both sides were everywhere.

At one point Bolan saw a group of about fifteen Lebanese soldiers walking along a road, an air of resignation about them. They were turning their backs on the war and simply going home.

15

Bolan left the rattletrap Saab and rounded a corner on foot in his search for the designated pub.

The time was 10:28.

The bar was located midblock on one of the streets that appeared relatively normal and untouched by the fighting. But even along there no one gave a second glance to the heavily armed soldier in blacksuit.

The businesses were mostly closed along the street, except for the taverns, which, as Zoraya had said, did a business almost as booming as the heavy artillery up in the hills.

Dozens of people in various stages of intoxication moved in and out of the pub in the ten minutes Bolan crouched around the corner of a building at the end of the block.

He recognized the Mossad agent and another man because of their sober intensity; this told him he had Uri Weizmann as surely as the guy's jacket matched the description Zoraya had given.

Bolan crossed the street and moved up the sidewalk, closing in on the Mossad undercover operative and his companion without letting them know it.

When they slipped into a Renault, Weizmann in the passenger seat, his associate behind the wheel, Bolan slipped into the back seat behind them, the Beretta in his left hand pressed against the base of the driver's neck, Big Thunder ready to shred the man from Mossad.

"Let's talk." Bolan nudged Weizmann with the barrel of the AutoMag. "You start."

"May I reach for identification?"

"Slowly. Very slowly."

The man obeyed and held a thin leather packet open over his shoulder for Bolan to read.

The ID indicated he was Uri Weizmann, Israeli Embassy Staff personnel.

The silence grew louder inside the hot car.

Bolan read these men as unafraid, seasoned hellgrounders like himself. Their grim expressions were blank masks.

"You realize anyone seeing me flash my ID in this neighborhood would make sure the mob in this street tore me apart," Weizmann snapped.

The driver grunted assent.

"The three of us would be dead."

"So put it away." Bolan pulled his guns back from the neck of each man, lowering the pistols but keeping them aimed below window level. "You're still covered." Bolan nodded to the driver. "Who's your friend?" he asked Weizmann.

"I am General Chehab," the Arab at the wheel said.

"Of the Lebanese army," Weizmann added. "The general is in charge of presidential security. Naturally, when Zoraya told me you had information on a plot to assassinate the president—"

"I insisted on coming along," Chehab rasped.

"There have been two attempts on the president's life in the past month. Syrian agents, trained by the Bulgarians."

"So this time they got someone else to do their dirty work," Bolan said. "Last night at an Iranian base in Biskinta I found blueprints of the presidential palace at Baabda."

Chehab lost his cool. The Lebanese officer spun around and eyed the big guy in the back seat.

"My Phalangist units monitored the fighting. You?"

"With a little help from the Syrians. They don't want your president assassinated any more than you do. Not right at the moment, anyway. That's why Strakhov is in Beirut."

Bolan concisely related the developments regarding General Masudi and the Disciples of Allah and what had transpired during the battle for the Iranian Revolutionary Guards' base at Biskinta.

"We know of the Disciples, of course," the Israeli said when Bolan had finished. "Masudi most likely told the truth before this Major Kleb killed him. That was only one cell of the Disciples you eliminated at Biskinta."

"American, I thought you had something new to tell us," Chehab snarled at Bolan.

"Slow down, General, we're not that friendly yet," Bolan snapped. "Are you a general in the army or the Phalangists?"

"At such a time as this, American, the two forces are much as one."

"I learned something else at Biskinta," Bolan told

them. "An unmarked government car was seen leaving the Iranian base before the Syrians attacked. A car... like this one."

The general's poker face remained inscrutable.

"Are you suggesting anything in particular?"

"I'm suggesting you get on it, General. Trace and verify the whereabouts of all unmarked government cars last night. You have the clout to do that?"

"But of course."

"Then that's all I've got for you, so you can leave us and begin now while I have a few words with Uri in private."

Chehab got a tightness to his eyes, but he held himself in check and glanced at Weizmann.

"Do you wish to be left alone with this, uh, gentleman?"

Weizmann glanced at Bolan's pistols.

"I don't seem to have much of a choice, General. But yes, do as Mr. Bolan suggests. And of course keep this extremely confidential. A government car...that means we're dealing with someone on the inside. But I think I shall be safe here. We're on the same side, Bolan and I, after all."

"As you wish," the general grumbled.

Chehab left them.

Bolan watched the Arab get out of the Renault and amble down the crowded street.

"Don't be too sure about the same side. The Phalangists have committed as many or more atrocities against civilians as the Muslims in this war."

"It is difficult to take either side," Weizmann conceded. "There are no good guys."

"Except maybe the guys who are trying to put a stop to it."

"Like us, eh? And is that what you wish to discuss?"

"Let's settle something first, then maybe I can dispense with this." Bolan motioned with the AutoMag still aimed at the man who called himself Uri Weizmann. "Your orders from Tel Aviv are that I'm top-priority TOS. Terminate on Sight. Your showing up to sit over in that pub and wait for me for half an hour, just the two of you, no backup, calls for an explanation and a good one."

"If what I have heard about you is true, Mr. Bolan, you will understand when I tell you that Chaim Herzl and I had been friends since childhood. Chaim saved my life twice. I never had the chance to repay him and now he is dead. Zoraya told me all about it when she called. And so I must repay Chaim some other way.

"It is ironic, is it not, that we do not know which side actually killed Chaim in the cross fire between Phalangists and Muslims. Does it matter, really? I don't know if Chaim knew the truth about you, or if he but followed his Uncle Yakov's instructions without question. I know he respected his uncle greatly.

"But Chaim did understand that only swift, decisive measures can achieve lasting peace in Lebanon and prevent more slaughter at this late date. I have been stationed in Beirut with Mossad for three long years and have seen the situation here only deteriorate. Perhaps it is time the Executioner got here. You may already be too late."

Bolan holstered his weapons.

"It's never too late." He reached for a pack of cigarettes, offered Uri one and lit them both. "Do you know where Zoraya is now?"

"I thought with you. She said she was returning to be with you when she telephoned me to arrange our meeting."

"I'll need help, Uri. Strakhov has called a meeting of the Muslim factions for noon today at the base at Zahle."

"I already know of this, my friend." Weizmann smiled. "We have our ear to the ground, as you Americans would say. In fact, the information has already been processed. The base at Zahle will be leveled by Israeli aircraft at precisely 12:10. Approximately one hour from now."

"Then you've got to pass on additional intel and call off that strike."

"Call it off?"

Bolan told Weizmann what happened to Zoraya's uncle at the garage. And his thoughts on what could have happened to Zoraya.

"If the Syrians have connected her with you and Chaim and me, then the Russians have her," said Bolan, "probably at Zahle."

Weizmann frowned.

"I'm not sure I can do it. Get the Israeli air force to call off the air strike, I mean."

"The people Strakhov is bringing together could still escape," growled Bolan. "An air strike is too chancy. I've got to hit that summit meeting and make sure every damn one of them is dead. I have the chance to disassemble their entire infrastructure and that would cancel their effectiveness long enough for some real peacekeeping negotiations to take place."

"And the fanatics of the Arab Christians?" asked Uri. "The Phalangists have run wild, massacring every civilian in sight, many times after ceasefires have supposedly taken place...as you yourself pointed out."

"Squeeze every source you've got and pin down the government car that showed up at Biskinta last night," said Bolan. "Tap your pipelines into Syrian and KGB intel sources. Strakhov is working it right now, and it could move up standard channels before they realize how important it is."

"And you? What of the Executioner?"

"I told you. I hit the Russians and the Syrians at Zahle. And I've got to find out what happened to Zoraya. She's done too much for me just to write her off now. Do the Russians and the Syrians have her? Or is she working for them?"

Weizmann's frown deepened.

"You have reason to suspect that? It seems rather coldblooded considering what she has done."

"Hot blood gets you killed at a time like this, Uri. You sound like you might be in love with Zoraya yourself."

"That...that's ridiculous," the Mossad man bristled without much conviction. "I—I am concerned about her. Yes, of course I am...I don't know...." The indignation faltered. "Perhaps—"

"Some other time," growled the big guy. "I know what you mean. Every man who's ever met that lady has probably fallen a little in love with her. Some women are like that and she's one." He saw no reason to tell Uri of Strakhov. "There are stakes in this that you don't know about and I don't have the time to tell you. There's only time now to do it. Will you help me take these warmongers apart or not?"

Reason won the Israeli over.

"I will do what I can, certainly.... Your points are well taken. I may be able to delay the air strike perhaps a short time, perhaps not, but I'm afraid that is all."

"It will have to do," the Executioner said. "I need a way onto that Syrian base. The site will be vacuum tight after what happened this morning. Is there any possible way your Mossad connections could get me on base for what I have to do?"

Weizmann nodded thoughtfully.

"Yes, but it will be extremely dangerous."

"What in Lebanon isn't?"

16

Bolan left Weizmann and returned to his Saab, which was parked nearby. He checked below the car and under the hood this time for explosives, but found nothing. Then he climbed in and gunned the Swedish relic to life. He consulted his map for the most direct route to the Druse militia position in west Beirut.

Time had run out.

The summit gathering of insurgents called by Strakhov would be getting under way at the base at Zahle within the hour.

Bolan had the in he needed, thanks to Uri Weizmann, who had broken all the rules of his organization and training to avenge a friend's death... and maybe because he was in love with the friend's lady.

All that mattered now was that time *had* run out.

Bolan's knuckles shone white around the steering wheel. He bit off a curse at every delay he encountered through the bustling streets of this sector.

His destination: the Druse militia position occupying what had been a small shopping mall, now concertina wired, the "liberated" shops functioning as offices and to billet fighters between rounds in the ongoing fight for the city.

The "Paris of the Mediterranean" throbbed and

echoed under a white sun to the sounds of exploding rocket-propelled grenades. The sporadic popping of Soviet-made rifles intermittently chorused the throatier staccato of heavy machine-gun fire. Most thoroughfares were clogged with civilians being forced steadily from the densely populated neighborhoods near the front line.

At one point Bolan crossed an untraveled side street that bisected his route. He happened to glance down the alley and saw something he didn't like. He yanked the steering wheel, upshifting, and came down on the tableau of three Shiite punks towering over a woman in dark traditional Lebanese garb. Huddled next to her was a boy of about eleven and they were both cowering against a pile of rubble, each clinging to two bottles of water.

The woman was pleading for her life.

The camou-clad militiamen laughed and lifted their AK-47s. The situation was ready to explode as sweaty nervous glances of anticipation darted from man to man before the barbarians opened fire. But when violence erupted in that street it came from the open driver's window of the passing Saab.

Bolan triggered the AK-47 he held across his chest, his right finger caressing the trigger while he drove with the left hand.

The blistering fusillade of automatic fire from the Saab pulped the three Shiite gunmen into flying shreds.

The woman and her son continued on with their precious bottled water.

Exiting from the alley, Bolan steered back onto a

principal thoroughfare parallel to the first and approached the shopping center commandeered by the Druse militia.

Again, the contrast of everyday life so close to the killing touched Bolan with chilling awareness.

Almost every other Lebanese he saw along his route carried or stood near transistor radios, listening obsessively for new developments.

Beirut buzzed with desperation.

Static firing, grenade and rifle sniping continued all along the nearby Green Line that divided east and west Beirut. According to the English-speaking announcer's voice from the Saab's dashboard radio, the conflict was escalating into severe clashes.

As Bolan listened, the broadcaster explained how Lebanese army armored vehicles were attempting to advance from the museum crossing point halfway down the Green Line but were being repelled in a fierce battle. The prize was the crumbling gutted tower and rubble heap of destroyed St. Michael's Church, where heavy fighting had gone on since the week before for control of the church. The army said it had captured the church and lost it and now wanted to recapture it.

Big deal, Bolan thought.

It had to stop.

Piles of dirt had been placed around the entrance to the Muslim militia headquarters to prevent counterattack by the Lebanese. But the ten-foot-high pyramids of earth actually helped Bolan hide the Saab a block and a half from the base entrance. From his concealed position he could observe vehicles arriving and leaving without fear of detection from the Druse sentries inside the base. The dirt piles blocked their vision.

At one point a tank lumbered out from between the mounds of earth. The Soviet-manufactured machine rumbled past the Saab. Bolan leaned sideways below window level, hidden from the observation window of the war machine or the driver's or gunner's periscopes.

The tank clanked on past and turned a corner, then rumbled out of sight, the crawler track clattering on pavement toward the Green Line and the fighting.

Before the tank's noise had faded, another vehicle emerged from the Druse base and turned in Bolan's direction.

The Executioner got ready, finger on the trigger of the reloaded AK-47 in case this wasn't the connection Uri claimed he could use to set up Bolan's penetration of Strakhov's headquarters summit.

The meeting would be the biggest gathering of terrorist warlords that a peace-bringer named Bolan, a soldier who cared, could ever hope to target for extinction.

A jeep with Syrian markings approached Bolan's position. It was driven by a Druse militiaman accompanied by a shotgun-riding gunman, his assault rifle pointed skyward.

The vehicle, much like the one Bolan had escaped in from Zahle a few hours before, upshifted past the Saab and this time Bolan did not hunch down but sat there with his AK ready to fire. But that proved unnecessary because the vehicle chugged by with neither driver nor soldier sparing the Saab a sideways glance as they drove past him.

As the jeep cruised by, Bolan recalled his parting conversation with Uri Weizmann.

"We have a man planted in the Druse militia," Weizmann had told Bolan before they split up outside the pub. "A driver. We've spent two years planting him. I can't afford to lose him."

"Your man will have time to pull out before the air strike."

"The driver and a soldier will leave the Druse motor pool at a garage they took over near to the area where the new recruits are billeted. The chauffeur is supposed to drive with the soldier to pick up Fouad Zakir, the militia's strategist and liaison with the Syrian command at Zahle."

The pair continued away from the Saab, away from the base, without turning off at the corner as the tank had.

When they reached the middle of the next block, Bolan pulled the Saab out from the curb and followed the vehicle at a discreet distance.

The jeep went a quarter mile, then the wheelman steered onto a several-square-block wasteland of completely gutted, devastated buildings that happened to be well behind the lines of heavy fighting.

The duo pulled over to what had been the curb of a trashed zone.

Bolan drove toward the jeep and could see the soldier who had been riding shotgun jumping awkwardly out from the vehicle and trying to bring up his rifle to aim at the driver. Then a pistol in the driver's fist barked once just as Bolan came to a halt behind the jeep.

The pistol blast spun the soldier around into a death sprawl, a human discard amid the rubble.

Bolan left the Saab and knelt beside the man to relieve him of AK-47 ammo clips at his waist.

The driver of the jeep shot worried glances in either direction.

"Hurry. The area is heavily patrolled by both sides. If it weren't for the fighting elsewhere—"

"I read you," Bolan returned, and quickly climbed into the dead man's uniform. The outfit was ill-fitting, too small, but with Bolan seated it would not be noticed.

Bolan and the driver dragged the body out of sight of the road and hid it in the rubble. Then Bolan took the dead man's place in the passenger seat. The Mossad plant gunned the vehicle away from there.

"Well done, guy." Bolan thanked the Israeli behind the wheel. "I appreciate the help. And the risk you're taking."

"Control said it was essential. After Zakir reaches the base at Zahle, you and I will be expected to wait on base until their meeting is finished."

The driver steered along a deserted street.

"Will you be able to get off base without arousing suspicion?" asked Bolan.

The "Druse" chuckled.

"Their organization is a joke. I will drive off base once you and I split up. I will wait nearby until after the air strike. The soldier and I were separated in the fighting. At a time like this, no one will give much of a damn that he was found several miles away. The roads are full of deserters. I'll tell the same to my superiors even if there is no air strike.'' The Mossad man steel-eyed the American. "If Fouad Zakir survives this day my life will be forfeited.''

"I don't think your control would risk a man in your position unless he thought you'd come out alive," Bolan assured the guy. "Leave Zakir to me.''

The guy from Mossad braked the vehicle in front of a row of private residences.

"Gladly. He lives right here.''

The two "Druse" soldiers proceeded to collect the militia hotshot whose very presence passed them through two Druse checkpoints without problems. They entered increasingly hostile territory the farther they got from Beirut along the heavily traveled military road into the mountains toward Zahle.

Zakir emanated an arrogance that precluded conversation between himself and the chauffeur and bodyguard.

Bolan felt a gnawing anticipation in his gut with the ascending cool of approaching battle consciousness.

He had bought time for his Beirut payback. The anticipation had a lot to do with that. The payback, uh-huh, would be in the name of America's best, those much maligned, always-there fighting men of the U.S. Marine Corps, trained warriors who hold the front lines to keep American citizens and values alive and free.

Some people back home were starting to forget that—the soft, naive bunch who had lived too long in an artificial environment in which the reality of the world is concealed from view.

Bolan knew. He lived in a real world ruled by force. Diplomacy can function only if it's backed by force.

These were truths Bolan lived by and had seen proved many times in and out of the hellgrounds.

Yeah, he appreciated his fighting buddies in all the armed services. And he mourned with every American soldier and patriot their sacrifices made in the name of honor and duty, words that meant something to Mack Bolan.

Bolan equally appreciated the impossible task these guys had been saddled with: trying to maintain a peace where none of the participants wanted peace.

With the Marines' role in Lebanon restricted—wisely, Bolan thought—from taking any real, active role in the country's civil war, the U.S. fighting men had been unable to be anything but targets, and Bolan felt a sense of relief when they were at last ordered to pull out of a no-win situation.

Now was the time to pay back for all that, with interest, to a summit of cannibal greed heads who schemed to cut up Lebanon like a piece of rotten pie once their slaughtering stopped.

And Strakhov.

Bolan anticipated getting the KGB's Mr. Big in his sights and canceling a blood feud and a top savage that had both been around too damn long.

Bolan hoped he would learn the truth about Zoraya at Zahle, too.

The village clung to the mountainside exactly as it had that morning. But as the Mossad undercover man steered the military vehicle down the incline approach, Bolan could see that his hit on the Syrian base had caused even more damage than he'd had time to register before cutting out the first time.

What had been the two rows of tanks and rockets were now nothing but charred, mangled, indiscernible metal remains. The guardhouse that had abutted the gate had not fared much better, nor had the gate itself been repaired.

Soldiers were working on filling the crater in the middle of the road, made when Bolan had blown his way out.

As Bolan guessed, the security around the base had been tripled at least, both as a result of his previous attack and because of the summit meeting taking place.

Bolan and the driver kept their eyes straight ahead when the jeep stopped for a new officer of the guard to personally check Fouad Zakir's credentials.

The officer waved the vehicle through to the guards farther inside the grounds and those men stepped back, giving the Executioner clear sailing onto the base, which would very soon be a leveled death camp.

Weizmann had said he might be able to delay the Israeli air strike, nothing more. That meant Bolan could expect it within the next half hour, and once Israeli fighter planes started swooping from the sky to rain hellfire on this scene, he knew he would have to get out of there pronto.

The vehicle rolled forward onto the base.

The sentries closed ranks after it.

Like the jaws of a closing trap.

17

Uri Weizmann had just begun searching the second of three drawers in General Chehab's desk. Lieutenant Franjieh, the uniformed Lebanese military police officer standing attentively at the door, backed himself to the wall alongside the door of the unoccupied office, his 9mm Browning Hi-Power raised defensively.

"Someone is coming."

Weizmann forgot about the desk.

He had hoped to find corroborating evidence to what he already had, but what he had would do.

The Mossad man and Franjieh, the MP, had gained access easily enough into this Phalangist building on the outskirts of Beirut.

Weizmann cross-drew his H&K .380 automatic and held his ground.

A key turned in the lock. The handle twisted downward. The door opened.

The office staff had gone to lunch. Weizmann's Mossad ID had admitted him and Franjieh this far without incident.

General Chehab stepped into the office. The Lebanese officer froze when he saw Weizmann. The general's swarthy complexion darkened, the nostrils flared, but nothing more.

Chehab stepped all the way into the office and closed the door behind him. Then he saw the Lebanese officer holding the Browning Hi-Power aimed at him.

Chehab glared.

"What is the meaning of this?"

"You are under arrest, General," Weizmann informed him.

"On what charge?"

"I'll let Lieutenant Franjieh take care of that. He's all yours, Lieutenant. Get your men in here."

Chehab's hands clenched into fists.

"I demand an explanation. A couple of hours ago, Uri, you and I sat in a pub sharing a drink. Now this."

"Correct. We also sat in a car, if you remember, and a man we spoke with suggested the car we sat in might have been the same one seen leaving the Iranian Revolutionary Guards' base at Biskinta last night. That was when the Disciples of Allah obtained blueprints of the presidential palace in their plot to assassinate the president.

"Well, our friend...my friend...was right, General. We traced every unmarked government car, using Mossad and Lieutenant Franjieh's combined resources. The vehicle assigned to you, General, is the only one unaccounted for through routine investigation.

"And before Bolan and I separated this morning, he gave me the blueprints retrieved from Biskinta. Those plans have been chemically processed. Your fingerprints were all over them, General."

"A trick," the Arab snarled. "Why should you believe Bolan? His own kind want him dead."

"And why should we trust you?" Weizmann retorted. "You are commander of a government force, yet have your own office and are saluted by the men here at a Phalangist base. We know it all, you see. The military dictatorship you envisioned with yourself in command, militarily conquering and driving out the Syrian and PLO forces with a last-ditch counteroffensive with or without the Israelis' help.

"But you needed a spark to ignite more fighting among people already sick and tired of it, so you decided the stakes were high enough to arrange to get those blueprints to the Disciples of Allah. You planned to make damn sure you were nowhere near the presidential palace when that squad drove into it with a suitcase of dynamite and made the hit for you. You reasoned that because it would be a suicide mission for them, you'd be covered. Face it, General. It's finished. Your dream is over."

"And what do you intend to do with me, Jewish pig? I am a powerful man in this country. I could have all of these charges dismissed."

"That's up to the Lebanese," Weizmann growled. "I did my part to pay back a friend. All right, Lieutenant, take him away."

Lieutenant Franjieh blinked twice and squeezed the trigger. The Browning in his fist high-powered a tunnel right through the skull of General Chehab, point-blank, to splatter the wall with the life forces of the treacherous general.

"Justice is served," Franjieh said softly and holstered his pistol.

THEY HAD TAKEN KATZ to a squat clay farmhouse set in the wood line beyond sight of the road. The building was accessible only by a winding drive that ran smoothly until it met the shell-marked country road that led back to Acre and the Israel-Lebanon border. The dwelling was one of thousands of such nondescript structures that dotted the countryside.

The two CIA men, Collins and Randolph, had finished their interrogation of Katz more than an hour before.

"And now that you are through detaining me, I trust I am free to go?" Katz groused in his best experience-honed air of command.

He started toward the door.

The Israeli officer, Colonel Lenz, blocked Katz's path from the room, unfurnished except for the wooden chair where they had sat the Phoenix Force leader while they interrogated him; the scene had been like a bad imitation of the third degree in some old police film.

The only difference was that these guys played for keeps.

"I have my orders to detain you here until further notice," Lenz barked, a hand on the butt of a revolver holstered at his hip.

Collins, the Company man who had done most of the questioning, snapped, "You don't think you get off that easy, Colonel. You may be big news in the States but here you're just a guy who used Mossad for your own ends. And I'll bet they've got something to say about that. Stay put."

They left Katz with a guard standing at the door and two more sentries outside the window.

Two Mossad agents then came in to question him for another hour. Katz stonewalled and gave them just enough to impress and interest them. But the Phoenix Force boss did not kid himself, either. He had been one of their own kind for too long. They would consider torturing him for what he knew about Bolan, and quite likely with the blessing of Katz's own government.

The Mossad interrogators from Tel Aviv left Katz alone again. He knew they would be standing in the hallway on the other side of the door discussing, probably with a superior, the advisability of torture. Katz recalled spurts of electric current to the genitals as being a particular favorite in the Mideast with Mossad and everyone else.

He exploded into action.

He powerhoused from the chair in a blur of movement that belied the thickening waist of late middle age. He aimed at the guard by the door and before the man could shout any sort of warning, Katz crossarmed the sentry's rifle away with the powerfully swung prosthetic arm. The ex-Mossad agent caught the guard with a blow sharp enough to make the Israeli soldier unconscious for a while, but not to kill him.

Katz knelt and snatched the man's holstered pistol and rifle. Slinging the rifle across his shoulder, he took a running dive at the window of the room, his arms crossed over his face. He kept his body loose as he hurled himself through the panes, shattering the glass into a hundred fragments.

He landed smack into the two sentries posted outside the farmhouse. All three tumbled down in a tangled heap.

The guards were mere youngsters.

A seasoned fighter like Katz took them by the numbers, one elbow backward into a forehead, then the butt of the pistol snapped down to bop the other sentry on the temple.

Both men fell to the ground unconscious.

Katz hustled away toward a motorcycle parked alongside two unmarked vehicles behind the building. He figured the bike was there for running pieces of physical evidence gathered from interrogations at the Mossad house.

Katz heard shouts coming from the shattered window behind him—the Mossad men demanding him to halt.

The hell with them.

He ran past the unmarked cars first, glanced in hopefully, but saw no keys in the ignitions. He hit the jackpot with the motorcycle.

Katz leaped onto the bike from behind, heeled up the kickstand and kicked the machine to life. He turned around and triggered off three quick rounds at the guys in the window who had been about to fire on him.

He aimed purposely high, and the Mossad men ducked back inside long enough for Katz to do a wheelie out of there, feeding the bike so much power. He roared down the driveway before additional personnel around the "farmhouse" could be alerted to what was happening.

The motorbike whizzed along the smooth surface of the driveway.

Katz knew the difficult part would be when he hit

that shell-destroyed stretch of road leading back into Beirut. Right now he had no trouble controlling the handlebar accelerator with the prosthetic device on his right hand.

He thought he had a good chance. He didn't need to use the hand brake on that same side. If he had to stop he'd use the foot brake. But if the ride was too rough. ... He dismissed the thought. He only had to get around the first bend in the road. They would be after him within seconds and would easily overtake him in those cars.

But Katz only intended to clear the bend, then ditch the motorcycle and cut into the rugged terrain. He'd lose them on foot in the undulating hill region and find other transportation.

He had no intention of rotting away under Mossad interrogation while Mack Bolan fought alone less than two hours away.

Katz had gotten Mack into Beirut, and he would damn well give everything he had to help the big guy get out.

He heard car engines waking up in the distance behind him and the popping reports of gunfire after him. But no bullets from the direction of the house found their mark. He reached the end of the driveway and leaned into the turn, feeding the speeding machine more gas instead of less for the curve onto the main road.

He had to make it.

BOB COLLINS CROUCHED OUT OF SIGHT.

A Syrian supply convoy lumbered onto the base at Zahle.

When the trucks had passed, the CIA man returned to his prone position on a knoll overlooking the base. He focused his binoculars, waiting for something to happen.

Collins had parked his vehicle in the brush off the road. He was armed with a Colt .45 automatic.

As he had feared, the interrogation of Yakov Katzenelenbogen had yielded nothing, so Collins and Randolph had decided to play a long shot on intel Mossad fed them for coming in to help on the Katz thing.

The two CIA men had left the clay house where Katz had been questioned and started north back into the hellzone, their Company authorization passing them through Israeli forces happy to be rid of them.

Collins and Randolph had started toward Zahle, but only Collins made it alive.

They had driven over a land mine planted in the road, left by withdrawing Druse forces. The right front tire had touched the explosive, which tossed the agents' vehicle onto its side. Collins had rolled free through his open window and for a moment thought his partner had made it, too.

Randolph had not made it.

Collins had walked around to the other side of the car and had seen that the force had ripped away most of the right side of Al's body into an awful palpitating red gristle.

Collins had turned his eyes away, puked, then continued on until another means of transportation—a car he hotwired and drove— brought him to Zahle.

He raised the glasses and scanned the base again, shaking his head at the loss of his friend.

Al was dead, no rhyme or reason to it all, and Collins was surprised that he felt nothing yet but a kind of emptiness over the death of a guy who had become sort of a brother.

Collins had pushed on to Zahle where Mossad said a summit of terrorist insurgent factions had been called by none other than Major General Greb Strakhov of the KGB. It was probably taking place down there right now.

Collins had a hunch that Mack Bolan would not miss a chance like this to take on the eradication of the terrorist camp. The CIA agent also knew the air strike would descend on that base and would hit sometime within the next twenty minutes. And if Bolan is down there, he'll be caught right in the middle of it.

Collins in his tour of duty had seen what the Israeli Air Force could do to a target. And if the air strike did not get Bolan. . .Collins would.

Because a good agent named Al Randolph was dead and Collins was mad as hell about that.

And because those were Collins's orders.

Terminate Bolan on sight.

The CIA agent panned the base and the vehicles appearing with the principals of this emergency summit, like the jeep carrying Fouad Zakir, the Druse biggie and his militiamen bodyguards.

No sign of The Executioner.

Yet.

Come on, Bolan, thought Collins from his place of concealment overlooking the camp. Where the hell are you? Let's have some action. . . .

18

The driver of Fouad Zakir's jeep stopped in front of the Syrian headquarters building.

Zakir punched Bolan in the shoulder from the back seat and brusquely gave an order in Arabic. He pointed to the building where Bolan knew he would find Greb Strakhov.

Bolan did not need a translation this time, either.

The Druse commander wanted his "militiaman" to accompany him inside. That made sense.

Bolan knew the factions Strakhov had called for a summit maintained an uneasy working alliance with each other, but no one confused it for trust. The blood-spilling would continue between these groups after the imminent fall of the Arab Christian president's government to the insurgents. Unless Bolan hit them *now*; a head-shed hit to make sure. Then the Israeli Air Force could level what was left and Bolan *would* be sure.

First, though, he had to find Zoraya. *If* she was on this base; if she was held captive or...if she belonged there.

If. Maybe she wasn't there at all. Bolan had to find out before he made his collective head hit and...no, that would not be easy at all, even to a master of role camouflage.

The "militiaman" stepped from the passenger side of the jeep without another glance at the driver. Bolan made sure to position himself toward the rear of the vehicle so he would be facing Zakir's back. The terrorist boss debarked, snapped an order at the driver, then turned to march directly into the Syrian headquarters.

The jeep pulled away.

Bolan followed Zakir.

The Arab did not notice the ill fit of Bolan's uniform or if he did he did not care. And that made sense, too. The insurgents were a barely organized, ragtag force at best.

Bolan quickly eyeballed the place in the moments before he and Zakir left the merciless midday sun for the relative coolness of the same headquarters building Bolan had penetrated in blacksuit a few hours ago.

None of the Syrian regulars or Russian officers that Bolan and Zakir passed made any connection between the Druse bodyguard and the hell-bringer who had delivered these terrorists a taste of real terror. Bolan's olive complexion, the high cheekbones and firm, squarish jaw contributed to the effect.

The Syrians and Russians saw what Bolan the role-camouflage expert wanted them to see; they even expected a Druse gunman to wear an almost comically ill-fitting uniform. The Druse gunmen were considered bumpkins and worse by the comparatively well-disciplined Syrian army and their Soviet advisors.

Bolan's quick daylight scan of the inner compound around the building confirmed his first impressions from the predawn hit.

If they had a prisoner here, if they had Zoraya, she would be kept and interrogated in one of two places, since Strakhov would not have the HQ building to himself as he had when he brought Masudi here for questioning.

If they have Zoraya, she's in the HQ basement or over in that smaller building that looks like an office annex, Bolan thought. They won't question her in the ground or second level because Strakhov doesn't want the Syrians to know anything he could torture out of her. And they won't take her to the barracks buildings for the same reason, but to the low, sprawling building five hundred feet to the north of HQ. There would be more foot traffic in and out of a building like that, with its Syrian battalion emblem on the door, unless Strakhov has ordered the area cleared of Syrian personnel and has Zoraya in there.

Thoughts came to him of Eve Aguilar, a woman he cared for, who had fallen captive to his enemies during the Executioner's bustup of the Libya Connection when he had been John Phoenix. He had come to rescue Eve. . . and had not reached her in time.

The bastards had skinned her alive.

After a nod from a Syrian officer, Fouad Zakir stalked directly up the stairway to the second level, again with Bolan slightly behind him, toting the AK-47 over his shoulder by its strap in approved bodyguard style.

At the foot of the stairs Bolan noticed the stairwell continued down to the basement.

The corridor upstairs seemed crowded with soldiers armed with rifles that matched Bolan's, the uniforms and armbands running the full gamut of the Lebanese terrorist coalition. They were all here: the PLO, the Iranian Revolutionary Guard, Amal...and now the Druse militia in the person of Fouad Zakir, who barely glanced at the corridor full of bodyguards.

The Arab terrorist crossed to the nearest door, grunted some guttural order at Bolan with a motion that indicated he should remain out there. Then Zakir stepped inside and no one tried to stop him.

The meeting is already under way, Bolan deduced.

Strakhov would be in there now with the whole rotten bunch.

But first...Zoraya.

The men in the hallway barely glanced at the soldier who had accompanied Zakir as far as the door of the briefing room.

Bolan figured the various faction leaders would suggest facing each other across a table without being crowded by their bodyguards, yet the men in that room were not fools. At the first sound of trouble from within the summit meeting, that door would be burst inward under the power of these bodyguards, who would fall into place behind their leaders.

Some of the men in the corridor stood in small clusters, smoking cigarettes, conversing in subdued Arabic while more soldiers leaned idly against walls of the passageway. But every one of them had his assault rifle inches from fingertips and the low murmur of voices could not conceal the tension.

Bolan leaned against a vacant space of hallway wall and lit a cigarette. By the time he flicked out the match, the others had lost interest in him, accepting the image he projected.

After a couple puffs on the butt, Bolan casually ambled a few feet to the nearest stairwell leading downstairs—the same stairs he had used at dawn when his tracking of Strakhov and General Masudi brought him here. At that moment, Bolan gave the impression of the universal soldier in need of a latrine.

He rounded the corner from the others, and no one tried to stop him as he strolled down the stairs at the opposite end of the building from the Orderly Room.

He touched the bottom landing and found what he remembered from his penetration of the place that morning; a side door leading out, flanked by a stairwell that led to the basement level.

Bolan continued down the stairs until he came around a turn into the well-lighted basement corridor. His brisk authoritative step only fooled the two Syrian soldiers at a desk long enough for them to see this was no officer of any of the factions upstairs but a mere Druse peasant who had somehow gotten lost.

They watched the ''militiaman'' approach as if he wanted to ask a question. Then lightning-fast chops descended toward the unsuspecting troopers' necks. Both men died without a sound before they had even risen from their chairs. They sat back down with broken necks.

The absence of any other soldiers posted there told Bolan what to expect and he found it.

Nothing.

He raced from door to door of the basement, stopping to pick two of the four locks, but each room was unoccupied.

No Zoraya.

Bolan did not know whether to be encouraged or depressed, so he just kept looking, hustling back up those same stairs before anyone from above found the two dead men. That would happen before long, he knew, but so would the Israeli air strike. All that mattered now was getting to the office annex across from HQ, then hitting that meeting upstairs.

He came up the stairs and out of the building from the wing opposite the Orderly Room.

The atmosphere on the main floor hummed with activity, orderlies moving in and out of offices, Syrian field officers elbowing their way through clerks to deliver and receive vital intel on the heavy fighting that could be heard like distant thunder echoing through the valleys of the Shouf.

No one paid attention to the blue-eyed "Druse" who topped those stairs and briskly left the building, walking toward the HQ annex that had all the signs of having been cleared.

Bolan had to find out what that meant.

He burst through a side entrance of the squat annex structure and knew instantly that he had stepped into the trap he'd been striving to avoid since this mission began.

The annex had been cleared, sure, and there could have been more than one reason but the main reason had to be: *Bolan*.

Every exit out of the hallway Bolan found himself in had been plugged up with at least two Syrian soldiers.

There were about eleven men in all and every one of them was pointing an AK-47 right at the man in Druse militia garb.

Bolan sensed movement behind and felt himself being covered from outside, too.

The only man in civilian attire in the scene also held a gun, a pistol, pointed like all the others at the figure in the doorway.

Major Kleb, GRU, wore a satisfied cat's grin that did not make it to cannibal-hungry eyes.

"And now, Mr. Mack Bolan," Kleb purred, "I think we have you exactly where we want you."

19

Strakhov tried to keep his attention on the petty bickering between the factions, but without success.

The KGB chief sat at one end of the oblong table.

The representatives from the Palestine Liberation Organization, newly reorganized under Soviet sponsorship, and a representative of the Shiite militia sat to his right.

To the KGB man's left were the ranking Syrian general of this sector and the liaison officer from another Iranian Revolutionary Guard contingent.

Fouad Zakir sat at the opposite end of the table from Strakhov. The Druse VIP wore an oily smile that said nothing.

The squabbling continued over a minor point that had temporarily slipped Strakhov's mind, he noted with annoyance.

His stubby fingers pinched up the lemon slice from the saucer of his teacup. He found the sour taste of the citrus fruit to be exquisite—a relaxant of sorts that invariably allowed him the objectivity with which to appraise situations more accurately.

He sipped the tea but still could not get his mind back on whatever these accursed Arab desert rats thought to be so important they would die over their foolish religions. . .and of course to bid for power over others, such as Strakhov possessed.

He could not follow the conversation even though they had been ordered to speak in English, that damnable all-purpose language even Strakhov had to employ on occasion, a common tongue they all understood.

He could not stop thinking about Mack Bolan.

The thought of killing Bolan always brought a peculiar druglike warmth over the usually coolheaded Strakhov. He had wanted Bolan dead for a long time now and had utilized all the resources of his KGB unit and others, all without success.

The desire for Bolan's head had consumed Strakhov since the American had gone on that mission to steal a new Russian helicopter from Afghanistan and had killed the test pilot of the prototype helicopter.

The pilot's name: Kyril Strakhov.

Beloved son of Greb.

Kyril's mother had died giving birth to the boy, and Kyril's death severed something inside Strakhov that he felt might have been his last tenuous link to anything loving or kind or caring in this hostile world. After Kyril was taken from him, all Greb Strakhov could think of, all he ever thought of, was *Bolan* and *revenge*.

Killing Bolan, yes. . .and of course holding tight the reins of control over this wretched, barren corner of the world while these camel-dung eaters fought among themselves.

The security of Strakhov's whole organization was at stake and he knew it, all because Bolan had in his possession a masterlist of all KGB agents, operations and activities throughout the world.

The Executioner had to be stopped but until now, until this pit called Lebanon, the war of wits between Strakhov and Bolan had been cat-and-mouse ploys of strategic brilliance. Now, Strakhov knew he would be confronting his enemy.

Thirty minutes ago, just prior to calling to order this disparate collection of cretins, Strakhov had received word of intercepted CIA transmissions, not yet fully decoded but indicating that Bolan was operating in a wholly vigilante capacity with no affiliation to other factions in this area. With this news several things suddenly became clear to Strakhov. The notion of one lone commando penetrating this base before dawn today, of visiting such death and carnage, had to be considered anew in light of Bolan's presence. The American could accomplish such a strike, Strakhov knew from experience. And so he had ordered that GRU moron, Kleb, to plant a trap in the annex building of the Syrian headquarters.

Strakhov had versed himself well in the Executioner's methods dating to before, during and after Bolan's Phoenix period. The KGB boss half suspected Bolan would use camouflage to get himself onto this base. A man like Bolan could not ignore the obviously deserted annex. And when the Executioner stepped into that building the trap would spring tight and Strakhov would have Bolan. Greb Strakhov would avenge Kyril... very, very slowly. Strakhov expected revenge to taste most sweet.

He blinked such thoughts away and forced his attention to what had become a shouting match across the table between four of the five representatives concerning the division of Beirut once the fighting had stopped and the city was secured under Muslim control.

Strakhov stood abruptly and smashed down on the table a powerful fist that cut through all their camel dung and focused attention right where Strakhov demanded it: on himself.

"Enough! This meeting has been called to do away with bickering such as this."

The Iranian cleared his throat, the only one daring to speak back to the real power here.

"It is only that my people have fought and died for what is about to come to pass," the Iranian purred hollowly. "Is it not reasonable to expect some recompensation in the form of—"

"Brigand!" snapped the Syrian. "You were never asked to help, you fanatic. We—"

"Gentlemen, gentlemen," soothed Fouad Zakir silkily, without taking his eyes from Strakhov. "The Major General is quite correct. To bicker among ourselves. . . ."

The slimiest snake of them all, thought Strakhov.

"I would not think it necessary," Strakhov told them curtly, "to remind everyone here that I speak not as an individual but as a representative of the Soviet Union, and as such I do not offer you suggestions or options but orders."

That got their attention and Strakhov started to continue when an orderly knocked discreetly, stuck his head inside, then walked over to Strakhov's side. The man whispered the words Strakhov had been so eagerly waiting to hear. Now they fanned the warmth in him to a fire hot enough to burn a man to death.

"Major Kleb asks that you come immediately to the annex building," the orderly whispered in Strakhov's ear. "They have captured the man Bolan. Alive."

BOLAN NOTICED HOW COCKY Kleb had become in the hours since Bolan had seen him last, since this morning when Kleb had not known he was being spied upon. Bolan attributed it to the guy's abrasive mentality generally and the success of having shot Masudi to death despite the chewing out it got him from Strakhov.

Bolan still gripped the AK-47 by its strap over his shoulder.

With twelve weapons trained on him, he would have to wait for a break. To move now would be suicide. If they had wanted him dead, he'd have been fired on already by these anxious soldiers who hung on the GRU man's every suggestion.

Kleb kept his pistol steady on the man who had stepped into the trap. Kleb's moist smile said he savored this moment.

"Major General Strakhov will be with us directly." Kleb had dispatched an orderly to interrupt Strakhov in his meeting. "And now, Mr. Bolan, you will kindly drop your weapons and if you try anything untoward, I shall be forced to shoot off your kneecaps."

Kleb started to say something else.

An ear-piercing sound signaled the approach of jet fighter planes.

The first in a line of explosions started eating up the perimeter with bellowing chomps.

Bolan seized the instant. He crouched, reversing the AK-47 in the flash that every eye in that room, including those of Major Kleb, were wrenched fearfully from the American. Bolan opened fire on the nearest four men, pulping them to sprawled carcasses before the line of explosions quit. It ended only a few hundred yards from the annex building, the echoes swallowed up by shouts, then another high-keening fighter plane hurtled in low to blast two of the barracks to hell.

Some of the survivors in the annex turned and fled, preferring Israeli jets to the hell-bringer with the AK-47.

Two of the soldiers who stayed tried to bring up rifles, but the AK yammered some more on automatic and the pair were hurled back into a wall as if punched by an invisible fist. When their bodies finally came to rest, parts of them stuck to the wall, glistening red. Some of the same heavy-caliber projectiles blasted Major Kleb's kneecaps in bloody splats of gore.

Kleb cried out and fell to the floor, his pistol flying from fingers numb with the pain ripping through his every nerve end. He cried out again when Bolan knelt beside this terror merchant and pressed Kleb's throat to the floor with the AK.

As more jets flew low overhead and more shouts and antiaircraft gunfire and explosions rumbled from outside, Bolan spoke very calmly.

"The woman. Zoraya. Where is she?"

"Z-Zoraya?" the GRU man gasped. "Please...I cannot stand the pain!"

Kleb screamed hysterically.

"The woman," Bolan repeated. "Where is she, Kleb?"

"Th-there is no woman!" Kleb shrieked. "The pain! Please. . .*kill me!*"

Kleb lapsed into a quick word or two of Russian.

The Executioner twisted the rifle with a harsh yank across Kleb's throat.

The Russian died instantly with a broken neck and no more pain.

Well, he did ask for it, Bolan thought as he moved on.

The soldiers had scattered from the buildings that they all rightfully considered the main targets of the air strike.

Bolan exited the annex building in a dash toward the nearest entrance to the Syrian headquarters.

His instinct told him to believe Kleb's dying statement.

No woman, Kleb had said.

Zoraya was not on the base.

And that left the Executioner's main objectives: a summit meeting of terrorist cannibals on the top floor of the Syrian headquarters. And Major General Greb Strakhov.

Antiterrorist guns pounded vainly at the expertly piloted attack jets that swooped in from unexpected angles. Their strafing runs turned the Syrian base into a shrieking feast of burning death.

Bolan knew the chance he took by entering this building. But the stakes were too high for the Executioner to turn back when he could accomplish what he would when he hit this bunch upstairs.

Bolan had committed himself totally to establishing a crack in the wall of violence that had kept this country destabilized for so long.

This hit would accomplish a lot and no way could a man like Bolan walk away from such a responsibility.

He gained entrance to the headquarters building easily enough in all the excitement. Those staring and crouching every time a jet whistled by or an explosion burst saw a Druse militiaman hurrying back to his post to protect Mr. Zakir.

No one tried to stop "Druse militiaman" Bolan. He took the steps upstairs at a run. Halfway up the stairs he passed a window that overlooked the area separating the building Bolan was in and the annex where he had slain Kleb.

Strakhov, a Russian officer and two Syrian soldiers were hurrying into the annex.

Bolan kept moving up the stairs, gripping the AK-47. He could not run back and forth.

First the warlords of terror.

Then Strakhov.

If Bolan survived.

The confusion he expected in the meeting area from the air strike would work greatly to Bolan's benefit, as would the element of surprise.

He hit the top landing of the stairs on the run.

The banshee shriek of a jet fighter screeching by overhead as Bolan hit that top step suddenly gave way to a thunderclap that made him deaf for a moment.

All he could feel were the shock waves of an explosion that catapulted him into the air. Amid flying mortar, sound and blinding fury, he knew he was airborne, a direct hit on the building pitching him into what seemed like a yawning pit.

He did not know if he was dead or alive as the maelstrom swallowed him whole.

20

Bolan kept himself stuntman-loose. The force of the blast deposited him roughly onto his back, the momentum propelling him along the ground. The explosion had rattled him, but as far as he could tell there were no bones broken.

He rolled over onto his stomach, his fists still clenched around the AK-47. He brought up the assault rifle instinctively to firing position while he shook his head to clear the sense-tumbling reaction of having been pitched through space.

The Executioner sized up the scene in the hallway at a glance, choosing his targets, squeezing off tight bursts from the AK-47 at anyone with a weapon.

Sunlight flooded through a ragged gaping hole in the wall and roof behind him at the top of what had been the stairs, onto the grisly remains of soldiers caught by flying brick or shrapnel. Other men of the bodyguard force had been knocked to the floor and appeared stunned, a moment behind Bolan in reorienting themselves.

He targeted his first burst at those who had missed the intensity of the blast, the ones who now turned to face him, not sure if he was friend or foe. They death-jigged and toppled under the hail of automatic fire.

Then Bolan mowed down the ones who were just now realizing they were already dying. He took out three PLO hardguys with a stitching blast as they came through the open doorway of the meeting room where Strakhov's summit of death merchants had fallen apart into bedlam.

Bolan fed a fresh clip into the AK-47 and stalked into that room to deliver some long overdue tabs. With interest.

The savages in there had been in the hurried process of breaking camp, trying to escape the devastating air strike that seemed to gobble up the whole world outside the windows.

The rats were abandoning ship, all of them and their surviving bodyguards already on their feet and racing toward the door. But they checked their progress, reaching for hardware after hearing sounds of The Executioner at work in the hallway.

Bolan triggered the AK-47 before he came all the way through the doorway. He remembered this as the office he had crossed in the dark that morning during his first penetration of this base. They were all standing in various attitudes around the table, lined up like targets in a gallery, pulling guns.

The PLO man caught a row of flesh-exploders across his chest and toppled sideways into a Shiite. The slugs missed the Muslim militia chieftain's gut, but they tore apart his head and shoulders instead. Both men collapsed, crashing into the table together, spreading puddles of blood as the AK-47 spit more death.

A volley of projectiles nearly ripped apart the IRG

member at abdomen level, severing his head from his body when he doubled over.

General Abdel's successor, as commander of this base, forgot about his pistol and tried to shriek an order or entreaty to the doom-bringer in the doorway, but a burst from the AK silenced the Syrian savage rudely and permanently, and the officer fell atop the other bodies.

Fouad Zakir, the Druse terrorist mastermind, appeared unable to grasp the simple fact of what had happened. He gazed from among the bodies, still shivering in death throes, and squinted through swirling gun smoke into the diamond-hard gaze of The Executioner. Because Bolan still wore a militia uniform, the Druse warlord felt something could be worked out. The cannibal who sat in guarded safety to plan the massacres of so many now held a pistol, but checked tracking it upward. He dropped his pistol and he put on his best snake-oil smile and earnestly implored something of Bolan in Arabic.

The Executioner triggered another burst from the AK-47 and blew Fouad Zakir's oily face off the face of the earth.

Now for Strakhov.

Bolan retraced his steps out of the briefing room, halting only when half a dozen Syrian regulars charged up the stairs from the other end of the building. Bolan opened fire and some fell, the rest diving for cover.

Bolan started down the rubbled, half-destroyed stairs at this end of the building.

A jet, maybe two in tandem, thundered by low overhead, their whine magnified by the hole in the side of the building.

Two Russian attachés peered up from the bottom of the stairs, paused, confused for an instant at the sight of the man in Druse uniform. Bolan's AK chattered again and the flunkies toppled backward, leaving trails of body pieces that The Executioner avoided as he charged down the steps. His single objective now was to cross the killground to that office annex where he hoped to find and finish the king of the savages.

He got thirty paces from the Syrian HQ building when a Mirage fighter swooped in out of nowhere, slamming down a string of heavy cannon fire that chopped up the earth into geysering explosions, ripping through lines of men and equipment and buildings, advancing jet-fast toward Bolan as the pilot strafed the base.

Bolan dodged to his right toward a sandbagged antiaircraft gun position, the occupants of which were fully riveted, returning the fire at the hurtling aircraft. Their rounds missed, but the explosion where Bolan had been an instant before missed him. He dived into that gun nest, yanking out his combat knife and whittling away at the three men. Blood spurted everywhere as the flashing blade bit deep into flesh, slicing into vital organs, leaving the surprised trio sprawled around The Executioner.

He looked over the edge of the sandbags in time to see, through the clouds of smoke that drifted across the compound, a direct hit on the annex that Strakhov had entered minutes ago.

The building blew outward. Bolan ducked as timber, mortar and the fury-atomized structure and what was left was blasted with missiles, exploding into an inferno. Screams of agony rose above the noisy compound as the blast fried those inside.

Another jet screamed by. Bolan felt as if he could read this pilot's mind. The big warrior evacuated the sandbagged gun nest at full speed toward the perimeter, along with a number of fleeing Syrian soldiers and a few Russians.

This Mirage unleashed a series of explosive blasts that shriveled the Syrian headquarters into collapsing rubble like a windblown house of cards.

What was left of the flaming structure wobbled and tumbled at the same instant Bolan made it through the bombed-out concertina-wired perimeter. He climbed a knoll he knew would take him into view of the first curve in the road from Zahle after it passed the base.

He paused at the fence and spent a precious moment shedding his Druse militia uniform. A couple of passing Syrian regulars stopped to gape, then pulled up weapons. Bolan blew them away and continued over the rise, not knowing what the hell he would find. Bolan's heart hammered with the knowledge that he had accomplished at least one of the objectives of this mission. The terrorist infrastructure of the Soviet death dealers in this part of the world had been dismantled.

Strakhov could be dead; the building Bolan saw him enter had been blown up, but Bolan would not believe what he could not see when it came to Greb Strakhov.

In any event there was not much left alive or standing down there, Bolan thought as he viewed the ruins. The jets had shrieked off to the south, leaving behind charred, demolished ruins, as if some angered god had wiped the place away with one angry huff.

Bolan crested the knoll and slapped his last magazine into the assault rifle. There were no more fleeing soldiers in sight but he knew they were all around the rocky terrain beneath the cobalt sky and merciless sun. He came over the hill and saw the road.

And the Volvo that belonged to Zoraya.

Zoraya sat at the wheel, eyeing him anxiously.

Seeing her did something funny to Bolan, but he was not sure what.

''Mack! Hurry!''

Bolan had intended to. He charged down that slope toward the Volvo.

When he got within twenty paces, Syrian soldiers appeared from two different directions: five men across the road, closing in on the other side of the Volvo, and two approaching at a run.

Bolan lifted the AK in the direction of the five men coming at Zoraya from the lower ground beyond the vehicle. He squeezed the trigger, braced to ride the weapon's recoil. Nothing happened.

The damn thing had jammed!

Bolan threw away the useless weapon and pawed for the AutoMag, knowing he would not have time to take out all these odds no matter how good he was.

Zoraya opened fire with an Uzi submachine gun from the passenger side of the Volvo.

The five troopers had been distracted by the sight of the combat figure in blacksuit and had momentarily forgotten the lady inside the car.

The Syrians toppled under a hail of Parabellum flesh-eaters seeking targets in one prolonged fifteen-second blast.

Bolan swung Big Thunder on the two who had almost reached the Volvo from behind. He fired once.

The guy on the left jerked backward off his feet, toppling into shrubbery along the road.

Bolan readjusted his mighty hand cannon from its upward recoil, but before he could waste soldier number two, that Syrian caught a single high-powered rifle shot from someone other than Bolan or Zoraya.

The soldier pitched forward, the back of his head blown away.

Bolan crouched, scanning the surroundings for the source of that helpful fire, but no one showed himself.

"We must hurry!" Zoraya called frantically from the car. "They are everywhere!"

"Right as usual," Bolan growled. He slid behind the steering wheel. "Hang on."

The Arab beauty braced herself for the ride, the Uzi ready.

The big guy popped the Volvo's clutch and kicked up a swirl of gravel, getting them away from there.

21

Bolan piloted the Volvo on two wheels and a prayer around the first bend in the road—right into the path of an oncoming deuce-and-a-half rushing reinforcements to what remained of the Syrian base at Zahle.

Bolan pumped the Volvo's brake pedal so hard he thought it would snap, twisting the heap into a skid. The grinding of the troop carrier's brakes and the blaring of the truck's horn drowned out the curse that escaped Bolan's lips as the Volvo slewed sideways onto the shoulder of the road. The deuce-and-a-half shuddered to a stop, men pouring from the cab and the tarpaulin-covered tailgate to investigate.

Bolan tagged the two from the cab with .44 headbusters.

Zoraya squeezed off a tight blitz from the Uzi that riddled three soldiers attempting to climb from the rear of the carrier. But she missed the pair debarking from the other side, seeking cover behind a culvert alongside the road.

The shooting ceased.

"How will we get those two?" Zoraya whispered to Bolan when they were outside the Volvo.

Before Bolan could respond, two sharp reports crackled in the afternoon air, followed by the sounds of bodies toppling beyond sight of the drain.

Bolan scanned the countryside, trying to plot a possible trajectory for those kill shots. He gave up when he realized the shots could have come from anywhere. The terrain around the mountainside village was a sniper's paradise.

"We seem to have acquired a guardian angel," Bolan mused. "All right, lady. Ready to travel?"

"We have no choice," replied Zoraya. They returned to the Volvo, Bolan behind the wheel, and drove away from the truck and the road littered with sprawled bodies.

As Bolan wheeled the vehicle away from the site of carnage, many thoughts flashed through his mind with instant clarity. The realization had hit home the moment he saw Zoraya Khaled risking her life for him, trading shots with the enemy. An enemy would never have done that. Bolan knew his first gut reaction to this special lady had been right all along.

Her voice, throaty and sense-intriguing as always, broke into his thoughts.

"You must forgive me, Mack." Zoraya avoided his eyes. She popped another magazine into the Uzi. "I . . . lost control for a moment when I first saw you. I was so afraid you had died in the air strike. I warned my sister who cooks for the troops at that base. Uri knows she is a key source of information and told me so I could tell her in time for her to escape. But I wanted to help you. I did not want you to end . . . like Chaim. I thought . . . if you needed me—"

"Which I did. Thank you, Zoraya, but I'm afraid I've got some bad news."

"About my uncle, yes. He sent me out for supplies.

He thought since it was his business he could better draw attention away from where you were hidden if anyone came looking. I saw the scum leaving who killed him. Our own kind. Druse gunmen. I... slaughtered them. When I returned to the garage a few moments later...you were gone. But what of now? I do not understand...."

"For starters I'd better get us out of this country," Bolan said. "My work here is done."

He did not want to think of Strakhov. Not at the moment. He wondered if the KGB commander boss cannibal had been killed in that air strike. He had a hunch deep inside that he and Strakhov would confront each other again someday. But he saw no reason to lay that on the woman beside him who had already done so much.

"I have spent some time today arranging your withdrawal from Lebanon through my friends in the underground. Just in case your plans went astray." Zoraya smiled. "One cannot always anticipate the plans of Allah."

"You'll accompany me?"

He thought he knew her answer to that but he had to ask, and her response told him he had been right about her, yeah. This was one very special lady.

She shook her head without taking her eyes from the countryside flashing past.

"My place is here, Mack. You can see from here how the fighting in Beirut has ceased. The artillery bombardment has ceased."

Bolan had noticed.

"So no one can say Chaim Herzl died in vain," he

acknowledged. "His dream of peace may still come true. Maybe today."

"There is talk of the president's being forced to step down," said Zoraya. "Of negotiations for a new government to give more rights to Muslim citizens. My people must continue the struggle because we have no other choice and I must be part of that. I cannot leave my home."

And that was when Bolan saw the guy standing in the middle of the road. Bolan did not peg him as Syrian or Russian. He was wearing American threads, holding his ground in a gunner's crouch, a .45 automatic aimed at the windshield, at Bolan's head. He looked as if he would not give an inch, daring Bolan to run him down.

Bolan braked the Volvo into another abrupt sideways stop.

Zoraya's knuckles whitened on the Uzi.

"Do not stop! It is a trap!"

Bolan had already stopped.

As he stepped out of the car to face the man in the road, he whispered back into the car to Zoraya.

"He's mine. Don't shoot. Don't do anything."

"Mack—"

Bolan moved away from the car, out of earshot of her plea, to approach the man aiming the .45 at him. Bolan kept his pace steady, his empty hands well away from his holstered weapons. He stopped when he got close enough to discern the sheen of sweat across the American's forehead. He locked eyes with the man.

"CIA?"

The man nodded. The .45 did not waver from between Bolan's eyes, the gunner's crouch tense, like an animal ready to spring.

"Collins. You're Mack Bolan."

"That's a fact," Bolan replied in a monotone. "So what are you going to do about it, Collins? Do you know what I just did back there?"

"At Zahle? I saw the whole thing and you did good. But orders on you are to Terminate on Sight, buddy boy. I lost a friend today. I saw him blown to bits, and you're a part of the goddamn problem."

"I'm the solution to the problem," Bolan corrected. "I'm sorry about your pal. I've lost some along the way, too. It's that kind of war. But we're on the same side, guy. I've never fired on a comrade in arms. I won't fire on you and I won't have this lady fire, either. But if you saw what I did down there...I can do it again and keep on doing it where it counts until the vultures stop me, if they can. Or you can stop me right here and now and let them score the point. You know that's the truth, Collins. You decide the future."

The .45 drew its unwavering bead for another moment.

Then Bob Collins lowered the pistol.

"You're right, you know that. I guess the heat...all the killing, it got to me." Collins holstered the .45 and stepped from the middle of the road. "Okay, Bolan. Next time it won't be like this, if we eyeball each other again, but yeah, I saw what you did. This one's for Al Randolph. Okay, go do it again somewhere."

Bolan returned a curt nod to that, returned to the Volvo and drove past and away from the Company man without looking back.

The woman beside him touched Bolan's arm with feather-light fingertips, a look of concern from those smoldering eyes.

"You take great chances."

"I have a guardian angel," Bolan reminded her, scanning the receding terrain behind them reflected in the Volvo's rearview mirror, seeing nothing but Bob Collins returning on foot to his vehicle.

Bolan felt weary, but he felt good, too. He felt strong, stronger than ever in his belief in a better world as long as there were people like Zoraya in it; a reaffirmation of his dedication to the everlasting war of a soldier's life.

"Now then," he said to the lovely beside him as they rounded a breathtaking panorama of the Mediterranean stretched out to the horizon far below, "what was that you said about getting me out of here?"

YAKOV KATZENELENBOGEN lowered the rifle from its target, no longer telescoped with the cross hairs centered on Collins's head.

Katz had witnessed the brief scene between Bolan and the CIA man, who now climbed into a sedan and drove off in the opposite direction taken by Bolan and the woman in the Volvo.

A fresh breeze blew in from the sea, whisking away the clouds of war and letting the sun shine in on the city far below, battered but still standing, like its people.

Survivors with hope.

Katz watched the Volvo drive around the bend in the mountain road leading to the sea, and when the car disappeared he decided he would not follow it farther. The helping hand he'd given the Executioner and the woman had seen them far enough for the warrior in blacksuit to carry it for the touchdown.

Katz had worked his way across the Israel-Lebanon border using his knowledge of security along the frontier. Intel from the same sources about Strakhov's summit at Zahle had brought him here.

He hoofed over to his hidden vehicle parked nearby. He had his own withdrawal from "Paris of the Med" already mapped out and was not overly concerned with Mossad for the events at the farmhouse where they had tried to detain him. He had far too much dirt on his former colleagues stored away, waiting for release to the media, stuff that could topple governments east and west, ready to go out if they got to him.

Katz had gotten out of far worse scrapes than having Mossad angry with him. And with Hal Brognola, Stony Man Farm's White House liaison, batting for him, once he heard the Bolan side of the story, Katz knew he was already home clear. He would be ready for his next Phoenix Force mission by the time he reached the States.

As for worn, torn Lebanon, maybe things would work out for this beleaguered little nation, maybe not, but Katz figured Bolan and his country's military presence had done all they could.

The Executioner had defanged the cannibals of both sides, cooling an abyss within Hell itself where maybe reason could now rule the day.

As for the stunning woman glimpsed beside Bolan in

the Volvo, both already long gone down that winding mountain road, Katz did not shed much concern.

Katz knew Mack Bolan.

The Executioner could take care of himself.

And always would.

Damn *right*.

DON PENDLETON'S EXECUTIONER
MACK BOLAN

Sergeant Mercy in Nam...The Executioner in the Mafia Wars...Colonel John Phoenix in the Terrorist Wars.... Now Mack Bolan fights his loneliest war! You've never read writing like this before. Faceless dogsoldiers have killed April Rose. The Executioner's one link with compassion is broken. His path is clear: by fire and maneuver, he will rack up hell in a world shock-tilted by terror. Bolan wages unsanctioned war—everywhere!

Available wherever paperbacks are sold.

GOLD
EAGLE

JOIN FORCES WITH MACK BOLAN AND HIS NEW COMBAT TEAMS!

Mail this coupon today!